DUNGEON DADDY

JANE HENRY

SYNOPSIS:

His protection comes at a price: total submission

Rae

Imprisoned in my tower, shut away from the world, I lived in the pages of my books—and my fantasies.

Then he rescued me. Made me his.

He becomes the best Daddy I've ever known—caring yet stern.

Ryder

Kept captive her whole life, she's the perfect combination of beauty and innocence.

I bring her to Limits, the high-end, exclusive, members-only BDSM Club… my home.

Now she's under my roof and my protection.

I'll protect her, keep her safe…

And all she has to do is obey

Please note:

This is a work of fiction with adult themes. Please do not distribute without written consent from the author.

ACKNOWLEDGMENTS

Thank you to Shannoff Designs for doing yet another awesome job on the cover, to Miranda for your dedicated edits and unflagging support, and to The Club, the reader group who daily inspires, encourages and motivates. Thank you!

PROLOGUE

"Give me two months," Joel begged. "I'll have the money." His thin body and pale face, framed with shocks of blond hair, looking out of place in the luxurious leather chair.

Martel's lip curled in disgust. "And how am I to know you will?" he asked. "You know the penalty if you fail to pay."

"I know I can earn it," the young man promised, his eyes wide with desperation. "I will pay it back, with interest."

Martel sneered, leaning his stocky body back to peer down his pointed nose at the man before him. He inspired fear despite his short stature. His ice-blue eyes seemed to cast literal ice through the veins of people like Joel. He smoothed a hand over his short-cropped brown hair, folding his hands across his middle, his face growing harder.

"You're damn right you will. And you're using this money for a home for you and your new family? Not to buy that shit you used to shoot up your veins when you lived back in the city?"

Though Joel's cheeks flushed in indignation, he stood his ground. "I won't. I don't use anymore."

He'd come to Martel, the most ruthless loan shark in

Boston, so many times he'd lost count. He'd always paid him back, always with interest, and had never been subject to the gruesome, painful punishments Martel inflicted on those who failed to pay. "You know I'm good for it, sir."

Martel looked out the window, massaging his chin thoughtfully. "Hmm. Yes. But what will you use for collateral?"

"Collateral?" Joel blinked. "You've never asked me for collateral before."

Martel shrugged indifferently. "Times are changing, Joel. Interest rates are up." His voice hardened. "I've been double-crossed three times in the past month, and I've lost my patience."

Martel was only three years older than Joel, but had been born and raised in the inner city. He'd learned the art of "lending" from his father, who'd learned it from his father. A family business, one might say. He'd worked hard to prove his worth, rising to the top as the most respected loan sharks on the East Coast.

"I've got nothing to give you," Joel said, hanging his head. "If I had anything to give you as collateral, I wouldn't be here asking for money."

"You have your wife."

Joel's head shot up and his eyes widened. "You wouldn't," he whispered. "I'd never! You're... you're..."

"Sick? C'mon, Joel, you can do better than that."

Joel got to his feet, the chair clattering on the floor behind him. "I'd never let you touch her!" he said.

Martel frowned, his voice frigid with apathy. "You swore yourself not five minutes ago that there was no *need* for collateral, since you would pay me back."

"And I will!"

"Then *sit!*" The command was issued so loudly, Joel

jumped, then picked up his chair that had clattered behind him before he sat back down.

"It's only security, you see. Besides, if I give you a loan without the rest of the requirements, how could I be seen as a fair and just man to anyone else?"

Joel nodded, defeated, as Martel opened a drawer and removed a large stack of crisp one-hundred dollar bills. He licked his thumb and began to fan the money out, counting each bill into a stack. After a moment, he tapped and straightened the stack, then pushed it over to Joel. "There's your money," he said. "And I'll tell you what. I wouldn't want to touch your wife. She is, after all, yours. But since you swear you'll get me the money, I'll give you an alternative."

Joel licked his lips, eyeing the money. "Yes?" he asked, his voice a mere whisper.

"You'll get me the money, Joel. Won't you?"

Joel nodded, the cowlick at the back of his head bobbing up and down. "Yes, yes, of course."

"No need for me to *collect* from you, right? I'll have the money, with interest, and on time?"

"Absolutely."

"Fantastic." Martel pushed the money toward the eager man, and pulled a contract out of a desk drawer. He clicked the end of a pen, and handed it to Joel.

"Then sign here."

"But—but you didn't ask me for… collateral…" Joel's voice trailed off.

"Ah, minor details," Martel said with a wave of his manicured hand. "But honestly, it's not really necessary, since you'll pay me." His brow rose slightly. "However, let's make the stakes high, just so I can show everyone else I mean what I say, okay?"

Joel's eyes narrowed and he swallowed audibly. "Okay…"

Martel smiled a slow, wicked smile. "Then promise me

your child. Your first born. You'll never have to *give* me the baby, of course, since you'll repay your loan."

Joel's mouth fell open, and the pen clattered to the desk. Martel picked it up and handed it to the man. "Sign on the dotted line, Joel."

Four months later

Gretchen rested her shaking hand on the head of her newborn daughter nestled in her car seat, singing a lullaby, as Joel drove crazily through the wet, dark streets of Boston and out to the country. Now that she held her sweet baby, the threat of Martel's kidnapping her no longer seemed as implausible as it once did. When the baby finally drifted off to sleep, Gretchen sighed.

"Joel?"

"Yeah?"

Gretchen swallowed hard. "Exactly how much do you owe him?"

"Well..."

"The truth, please."

Joel made a choking sound. "One hundred thousand dollars."

The only response from Gretchen was a soft sniffle from the backseat.

"It wasn't just for the apartment, Gretchen. It was... it's been... more than that. But for years, I'd make it back at the casino, and pay him interest. It's just lately I've run out of luck."

"Run out of luck?" she asked, her voice raising in tenor. "You call it out of *luck?* God, Joel."

They rode in silence for a few minutes until she spoke from the backseat once more.

"You know they've been following us for the last five exits."

The car swerved, then came back to the center lane. Joel swore under his breath.

"And there's no escaping them. You know that. I know that. We can't fight them."

Joel was silent for a moment. "But we have to."

"Drive faster. Please." Her voice dropped to a whisper. "Drive as fast as you can."

The car shook with acceleration, the frame unable to bear the speed.

The baby began to wail.

RAE

I STARED down at the man on the floor in front of me.

The first real person I'd seen in ages—and *oh my God* a hot guy at that. A strong, muscled, monster of a man with a scuff of beard and a square jaw, dark brown hair that fell onto his forehead—literally *landed* at my feet, and I knocked him out? What had I done? I dropped the iron I held in my hand and knelt beside him to see if he was still breathing. The iron was heavy and my hands were shaking, and he hadn't gotten the full smack of it. Still, he lay unconscious.

How was someone supposed to check for breathing? I flipped him over onto his back and he groaned out loud. Okay, then. Phew. He wasn't dead.

I only meant to *stop* him. I hadn't meant to *kill* him. A goose egg rose on the side of his head, and I felt a moment of chagrin, before I reminded myself that he had totally deserved the whack to the head. Who scales the side of a private residency?

I had to call someone for help.

But who could I call? I couldn't call the police, since they were friends with my father, and if I called my father... I shivered and swallowed.

He would hurt him.

I pulled a copy of *Ward's Best Home Remedies and First Aid* off the shelf, and scanned until I came to the chapter entitled "head injuries." Quickly flipping to the right chapter, I scanned the instructions.

Keep the person still. Ok well clearly, I could do that. He wasn't going anywhere.

Keep the injured person lying down and quiet. Again, not a problem

Elevate the shoulders and head. Hmm. I looked around my room and figured the huge pillow by the window where I read would work best. I lugged it down, which was no small task given that it was pretty enormous, and I tossed it to the floor, lifted his head, and placed it on top.

Stop any bleeding. Frowning, I looked as closely to his head as possible but there was no blood to be seen.

Apply ice once the bleeding stops. Well, that would entail having to go down to the kitchen, which would mean I'd have to take my eyes off of him. Nope.

Watch for changes in breathing and alertness. Alright, then. I sat cross-legged on the floor and stared. And stared. After a little while, I poked his foot. "Mister?"

He grunted and shifted. It was at that point it occurred to me that when he *did* come to, he could react violently or in anger, and it would be smartest to be sure he was properly tied up. Quickly, I got to my feet and ran to my closet, grabbed two thin belts from a hook at the back, and came back to him. I knelt, looped one belt around his ankles and another around his wrists, and pulled them tight, then fastened them.

There. He was nicely secured now, and I could watch for

changes in breathing and alertness easily. It was a boring wait, so I grabbed my copy of *Jane Eyre* that had fallen to the ground when I grabbed the pillow, and flipped it open to the bookmarked page. I had just gotten to the part in the story when Jane arrives at Mr. Rochester's home. I was so immersed in my story, I didn't hear him stirring until I heard a gruff, "What the hell?"

I dropped the book. "Oh, hi," I said, crawling over to see him. "You really startled me. Are you okay?"

He blinked, his eyes squeezing tight in pain, and he tried to move a hand to his head but they were still held together by the belt.

"Am I *okay?*" I swallowed hard. His voice was low, deep, and a little husky, and his sharp tone did strange, wonderful things to my body. I drew closer.

"I have no idea. What happened? Why am I on the floor? And why the *fuck* are my wrists tied like I'm some sort of criminal?"

"You *are* a criminal."

He frowned, his brows drawing together angrily. "What? No, I tried to rescue you!"

"Rescue me! From what? I was reading by moonlight in the most comfortable seat in the house and the next thing I know you're scaling the side of my home like a—a—ninja!"

He groaned and his head fell back. "Like a ninja. *Jesus.* I heard you scream and I was afraid someone had hurt you."

I felt a teensy bit bad at that point. That was sort of sweet of him. "Oh. I tripped and it startled me and I fell."

"Oh? What the hell did you hit me with, anyway? And why am I still on this fucking floor?"

"You really should watch your language."

"I'm on the *fucking floor* and you're holding me hostage like Misery or something."

"Misery?"

He shook his head, but the movement caused him to wince in pain. "Forget it. Listen... what's your name?"

"Rae. Well my full name is Rowena, but only my father calls me that." I couldn't bear to be called Rowena.

The words left my mouth before my father's admonition came to mind.

Never tell a stranger your name.

He'd ingrained it in my head from my youth, but I'd been secluded now for so long that I hadn't remembered to heed his warning. My cheeks flushed and I wished I could take it back.

"Rae?"

"Yes," I whispered.

My father would *lose his mind*. He'd lock me in my room and call his guard to come, the men who carried guns and dragged full grown men into my father's office.

I chose to remain ignorant of what they did in there.

"And your name?"

He grunted. "Ryder. Nice to meet you, Rae. Now unfasten my hands. This is getting really fucking uncomfortable."

"Language."

"My goddamned hands!"

I shook my head. "How do I know what you said is true? You trespassed on my property and I defended myself." I paused, and tried to look stern enough to cover my bluff. "Do you want me to call the police?" I wouldn't, but I wondered if the threat would help any.

He frowned at me. "You do have a tendency for the dramatics, don't you?"

I shrugged. "Comes from reading a lot, I suppose."

His lips pursed. "I suppose. So tell me again why you've got me bound here? We've already established I'm not a burglar, right?"

I squirmed. "Well. Not really, but okay."

DUNGEON DADDY

"For God's sake, I just came up to see if you were okay!"

Now that he was no longer unconscious, I suddenly became very, very aware of the fact that there was a man sitting in front of me, an angry, very attractive man. He was older than I was, by maybe five or six years. He had longish chestnut-colored hair, sky blue eyes, and a short, dark beard, and a body much, *much* bigger and stronger than mine. His face looked both friendly and stern at the same time

"I'm fine," I said absentmindedly, trying to decide what to do. If I let him go, he could hurt me, though he didn't really seem the type to hurt a woman. After all, he'd come up here to save me, supposedly. If I kept him, and my father found out I'd entertained a visitor—especially a trespasser like this—there would be hell to pay. But he was too big for me to move on my own, and he couldn't exactly lie on the floor of my bedroom propped up on a pillow for the rest of his life.

"Fine," I said. "I'll unfasten your hands. But if you do anything funny, I swear to God I'll hit you with the iron again."

He exhaled angrily and narrowed his eyes at me, his deep voice making me shiver. "I'm not going to do anything funny, but if you try to hit me with the iron again I'll whip it out the window."

"That's supposed to convince me to unfasten the strap?"

His eyes narrowed to slits, his voice a low command. "Unfasten my wrists."

My hands shook as I reached for the belt buckle. I'd never been so close to a man before. My father was the only man I'd ever met, and he only spoke to me from a distance. We never hugged, and he never touched me.

I wondered what it would be like to be touched by someone.

"That's a girl," he said, as the belt fell away and he flexed his wrists, then he undid the belt at his feet. He was so big, so

11

strong, that my mind immediately began to play tricks on me. What would it feel like if he… if he *did* overpower me? If he held my wrists in his strong grip, pinned me down, and took control?

Oh, God. I had to get a grip. I swallowed hard.

His murmured approval sent a shiver down my spine I didn't quite understand. I blamed my years of perusing every romance novel I could get my hands on for fostering these romantic notions.

Yeah, that was it.

"Christ, my head hurts like fucking hell."

He sure had a mouth on him, but I didn't admonish him this time. I did feel a little badly for the iron incident.

"I'll get you some pain relievers."

"Are you alone here?" he asked, stumbling a bit as he walked behind me, but he quickly righted himself.

"Um. No," I lied, badly. "I have a maid downstairs and a cook who lives here, as well as a butler, a driver, and a groundskeeper." We'd had all those people over the years but one by one my father let them go and now I was often alone.

"They all live here?"

I nodded, not meeting his eyes, as I led him to the bathroom in the hallway. I hated lying, but sometimes it was a necessity. When you lived with someone like my father, you learned this.

"They do, yes." My voice sounded unnaturally high. "In fact, um, I'm quite surprised none of them came upstairs to see what the commotion was."

He didn't respond, as I pushed open the door to the bathroom and retrieved the bottle of pain reliever from the medicine cabinet. He grunted his thanks, shook a few into his palm, and swallowed them dry. Yuck.

"Would you—can you tell me why you're here?" I asked,

leaning against the sink. He owed me at least this explanation.

He leaned against the wall, wrapping his hand around the side of his head as if to stop the pain. "I was traveling along the main road, and I got a flat tire. Couldn't see a damn thing, and my spare was flat. I had no cell signal. So I walked until I got here, and knocked and knocked on the door." He frowned and his voice dropped. "Awfully strange with all that staff no one answered the door."

Oh. Oops.

"They're all asleep," I said in a rush.

He raised a brow. "All of them? Even the ones who guard your estate?"

I didn't answer.

"I really just need to get out of here," he said. "Can I just use your cell phone?"

"I have no cell phone." Another lie but with a thread of truth. I had one, but he couldn't use it. It was only to be used in case of emergency, and my father would track any call I made or received.

He blinked. "No cell phone?"

I shook my head.

"Do you have... a landline?"

"I... we have one, but it's in my father's office, and I'm not allowed in there unless it's an emergency."

His brows shot up and his mouth dropped open, then after a moment he closed it and stared at me. "Okay. So. What exactly would constitute an emergency?"

It was a good question. "I suppose if I needed to reach my father."

He nodded slowly. "And my car being stranded by the side of the road isn't an emergency."

"No." Any calls made on my father's line would be tracked by him, and he'd know I had someone over at the house. I didn't want him to know… yet.

He frowned. "So what exactly am I supposed to do? No one on your entire staff has a cell phone? No one has any way of reaching civilization?" I watched as he scanned the bathroom, looking over the pile of plush towels, the huge oval mirror over the sink. "A place like this, and you guys don't have a phone?"

I shrugged. "Would you like something to eat?"

RYDER

WHAT KIND of bizarre fucking place had I found myself in?

The chick was lying about the staff. I was pretty sure she was the only one here, at least for now. I felt like I'd wandered onto some sort of sinister B-level horror flick. Just about the only thing that didn't creep me the hell out was *her*. She was weird as fuck, but it was a sort of endearing. She was also absolutely stunning.

I took a moment to really look at her as she led me downstairs. A full head of very, very long honey blonde hair hung past her waist, twisted into a thick braid. She was petite, with a slender waist and full hips that swayed while she walked, and a gorgeous, heart-shaped, very spankable ass. A cute little pair of glasses rimmed in gold perched on her nose, and her lips were lush and full. She wore a pair of faded jeans that flared at the bottom and a faded dark purple tank top, her feet bare, her entire presence reminiscent of some sort of hippie. And yet, it was cute.

"So who's your father?" I asked.

She didn't respond at first. Her voice was lower than I'd expected, a bit husky when she spoke, edgy even. I had a feeling when push came to shove, the girl could hold her own. "I'm not really supposed to talk about him."

Creepy.

"Alright, then," I said, annoyed at her evasiveness and how powerless I was in this situation. "You seem sort of alone here." She froze on a landing between the first and second floors and swung her gaze to meet mine, her full lips parted a bit. "I don't talk to anyone. He says the outside world is a terrifying place to be, filled with strangers who will hurt me." Her brow furrowed. "Will you hurt me?"

"We've covered this," I said, annoyed now. "*No*. I won't hurt you. He tells you lots of people would hurt you?"

She blinked. "Most."

Most? *Christ.*

"This way," she said, her voice hushed as we padded down the carpeted stairs. I followed. I'd find the phone.

I surmised she was some sort of homebound chick. On a whim, I decided I'd probe. "Are you here against your will?" I asked her. I had to. I couldn't leave things well enough alone. I needed to know.

She paused and tipped her head to the side. "You mean… like a prisoner?"

I nodded. I expected her to deny it, so her response took me off guard.

"Well, I'm not allowed to leave."

What?

"Do you want to?"

Her eyes quickly glanced away and her head dipped down. "Sometimes, I do. Most days, yes. But I can't, Ryder. You don't know what he's capable of."

I closed my eyes briefly. "Tell me what you mean."

"How's your head?" she asked, evading.

Seemed I wouldn't get very far questioning her. "Still hurts like hell."

DUNGEON DADDY

She didn't respond, just pushed open a large door to the dining room, which housed a long table with chairs flanking either side.

Part of me wondered how the fuck I'd get out of here.

But another part of me didn't feel right leaving this girl behind, knowing she was being kept against her will. My years of training as a dominant made me want to protect her, keep her safe. But I'd have to observe carefully. She was like a wounded animal, and I wondered how she'd react if she felt cornered.

She fiddled around in the kitchen, pulling out mugs and heating up a saucepan with cocoa, milk, and sugar, whisking away. "What do you do for work, Ryder?" she asked, as steam rose from the pan. I'd never had cocoa made with anything other than powder from a packet.

"I own a club."

"Oh. Marshmallows?"

"No thanks."

She sat across from me, her long braid swinging in front, as she sipped her cocoa.

"What's your father going to do when he finds out I was here?" I asked. I knew the answer. I hoped the reminder of this fact would get her to find me a way to contact someone who could help me.

She looked away and didn't respond at first. Finally, she placed her mug on the table and slid it away from her, then she ran her tongue over her top lip, cleaning the little hot chocolate moustache she'd managed to give herself. I swallowed hard, my cock twitching as I watched her. God, what I would do with that pert little mouth of hers.

"I...we need to make sure he doesn't find out."

"How are we going to do that?"

"I know you can't use his phone," she said. "And you have to be gone when he comes home."

JANE HENRY

"What will he do if he finds out?" I repeated. She was naïve to think he didn't have this place tricked out with surveillance cameras.

Her eyes widened. "He can't find out, Ryder. I – I don't know what he'd do. He's never touched me. But the people he's brought into his office…" She swallowed. "They scream," she whispered. "They make terrible, horrific noises." She shook her head and closed her eyes. Her voice dropped to a whisper. "I've never seen any of them leave." She drew in a breath and opened her eyes. "He doesn't know I've seen any of this, and I choose to remain ignorant."

A cold chill crept up my neck, the hair on my arms standing on end.

"Don't get the wrong idea, Ryder. He's… he loves me, he just wants what's best for me."

Bullshit.

Still, I nodded. What kind of sick fuck was this guy? Was she saying this because she had some sort of twisted Stockholm syndrome?

She looked away and cleared her throat. "How's your cocoa?"

"Great, thanks." I finished it in one final gulp and slid the mug over to her. She took it silently, stood, and padded softly to the kitchen. I heard her open the dishwasher, and place the mugs in before she clicked it shut and came back out to me.

"Where's the rest of the staff?" I asked her. I needed her to tell me the truth. I needed to know what the fuck was going on.

She looked away. "You'll see them in the morning, I guess. Maybe… I will show you to your room. My father won't be back for a few days, and you can find your way home in the morning."

My room?

"Yes, that'd be great."

I'd wait until she fell asleep, and when she did, I'd find out where the fuck I was. I'd get onto a computer or phone that would get me in touch with Seth, and I'd get the fuck out of here.

She led me back upstairs to where her room was, and opened the door next to it, a small room with a few bookshelves and a single bed, simply furnished. "What's this room?" I asked.

"This is just the guest room, not that we have any guests. Make yourself at home." She frowned. "I've never really dealt with a guest before."

"You're doing great."

Her eyes lit up then, full of life and hope. "You think?"

"Oh, can you come here for a minute?" she asked, and then before I knew what she was doing she was right up in my space, standing in front of me, her large brown eyes looking into mine, her finger on my chin. My pulse spiked. I inhaled deeply, my cock hardening. Fuck. She was too damn close and smelled so good it killed me.

"Rae... what are you doing?" I asked her, completely taken aback.

"Checking your eyes," she muttered. "Need to make sure it's *okay* for you to go to sleep. Need to look at your pupils"

"Right."

"Stay still."

Her breath stirred across my neck. I covered up my shiver of arousal with sarcasm. "Hardly doing a jig here."

She snorted and lost her balance, falling straight into me. I caught her, her soft body pushed up against mine, and after I gently righted her, I stepped back.

It was dangerous here. I couldn't get close to her. Fuck, I wanted to, though. It'd been a whole year since I'd had a full-time submissive, and maybe six months since I'd taken a woman to bed. I couldn't stop my mind from wandering as the faint scent of lilacs and freesia enveloped me.

"So what's the prognosis, Doctor Rae?"

She snorted again, and I braced myself as if to catch her, which only made her laugh harder, a musical, contagious laugh that made my lips curl in amusement.

"I think you're fine, patient Ryder. But we have to be sure—"

A loud crash made us both freeze in place, a bang followed by a thump.

"Oh, God," she whispered. "He isn't supposed to be home yet. He's supposed to be in Ontario." Her hand splayed across her chest as she took in a shuddering breath. God, the girl was scared shitless.

"We don't know it's him," I said, my jaw set as I watched her reaction. I didn't care who the fuck this guy was. He wouldn't hurt her on my watch. "Let's go find out." I started to walk toward the doorway, but she yanked me back so hard I almost fell.

"No!" she said, her eyes so wide and panicked now I felt my own stomach clench in fear. My hands fisted, ready to protect her from whatever dangers threatened to hurt her.

"Relax, Rae, it's going to be okay. We can't exactly skulk around here when someone could have—"

"No. Please!" Her gaze flitted away from mine, taking in the room. "God, oh *God*. Where can I hide you?"

"Hide me? I don't think so." I huffed out a humorless laugh. I was ready to defend her, no matter who or what posed a threat.

She grabbed onto my arms. "Listen, Ryder. You have no idea. If he saw that you'd broken into our house—" Her voice rose in pitch as if she were on the verge of hysteria, until finally I grabbed her by the arms and gave her a firm shake.

"Stop!"

She blinked, but stopped, her chest rising and falling with rapid breaths. At least I had her attention.

"Now sit down." I ordered. Years of experience as a Dom, and I knew how to take control. I pointed to a chair in the corner of the room.

"What are you going to—"

"Sit!" I hissed in case it was her father out there so he wouldn't hear us. Thankfully, she obeyed. I took in a deep breath, then exhaled slowly. "This is what we're going to do. You're going to stay here. I'm going to see who that is. I'll go slowly and carefully so whoever's down there doesn't see me, and then we'll figure out plan B. Problem is, you say he's supposed to be in Ontario, so I need to be sure there isn't an intruder. Okay?"

She nodded wordlessly, her lips clamped between her teeth.

I pointed at her. "You. Stay. *Here*. Got it?"

She nodded again, and this time her eyes reflected something else, but I couldn't quite figure out what.

"If he is here, he'll go straight to his office. It's his routine. He never veers, ever. It's down on the first floor."

I nodded, then left the room and padded along the hall, taking in every detail, looking for signs of movement or something out of place, but everything was quiet, and the sound had come from below us anyway. I moved stealthily to the top of the stairs and crouched down, looking through the rails, prepared to hide in the shadows if I saw movement, but I saw nothing at all.

Once I'd observed from the top of the stairs for a full minute, with no sign of anyone else below, I stalked down the stairs, staying as low as I could to avoid detection. I made my way back to the dining room but again, the entire room lay in stillness. I had to get to his office, where she said he'd be if he'd returned home, but the door was shut fast and when I looked under the door frame, it was dark. To the right of the study door was a little strip of windows, and everything was immersed in darkness.

I retraced my steps back to the kitchen, and it was then that I noticed something dark on the floor. As I drew closer, I realized it was only a vase, shattered, glass marbles scattered all around it, the silk flowers askew. Looking up above the vase, I noticed a window open, and an orange and striped tail slipping through the opening.

Mystery solved. I located a small broom and dustpan in a utility closet in the kitchen, swept up the broken glass, and piled it all in a paper bag. I would ask Rae what to do with the mess.

Satisfied that we were still alone in the house, I trotted back upstairs, taking them two at a time, looking around when I hit the top stair for one more final time to make sure I'd missed nothing. But all was still. When I entered the room where she waited, she still sat where I'd directed her to stay, her knees drawn up to her chin now, her long braid hanging to the side.

"Nothing down there. I found a broken vase, an open window, and a furry culprit."

Her eyes crinkled around the edges as she smiled and lifted her chin off her knees. "It was Starburst?"

I shrugged, feeling the fatigue in my bones now, ready to get some sleep. "Is that the name of a cat with an orange-striped tail?"

"Yup. She loves to prowl around late at night, fancies herself some sort of guard kitty. Protects us from mice and other such dangerous rodents. She broke the vase?"

I nodded. "I cleaned it up a bit, but left the broken pieces for you to put away. Not sure if it was sentimental or something and worth trying to fix."

She shook her head. "We don't have much in the way of

sentimental things here. It's fine." Unfolding herself from the chair, she stretched and yawned, her big brown eyes squinting shut, then she stretched her arms up over her head. "Thanks for checking, Ryder."

"Sure." I couldn't help myself. My eyes roamed over her gorgeous curves as she stretched. "Thanks for being a good girl and obeying my instructions."

Her gaze flitted away from mine for a moment while she sidled up a little closer to me. She turned back to me, her eyes alight with curiosity.

"So." She cleared her throat. "What would you have done if I hadn't?"

I shifted, hiding the sudden arousal that licked through me, my cock hardening at her low, husky question. It was odd, coming from a sheltered girl like her, but I knew what she was after.

"What's that?" I wanted her to repeat the question.

"If I… hadn't obeyed," she said, a bit of her bravado fading now, and she nervously twisted her braid. "What would you have done?"

"If you were mine? I'd have spanked your ass," I said honestly, gauging her reaction. Her eyes widened, her cheeks pinking as I crossed my arms on my chest. "I was investigating to keep you safe, and I wouldn't have been too impressed if you didn't listen."

"And if I wasn't… yours?" she whispered.

I smirked. "I wouldn't recommend you try me."

She observed me for a moment, then shook her head, as if to clear her mind. "The closet should have everything you need, your linens and towels, and in the morning, we'll see about contacting your friend or something."

"Thanks."

"Sure thing," she said, and she shut the door with a bang.

What the hell was that all about?

I sat on the edge of the bed and removed my shoes. It was ridiculous, a guy like me, taken with a girl who was some type of... captive. How had I found my way here?

How would I find my way out? I didn't like the idea of leaving her alone.

I listened at the door until I heard no more sounds from her bedroom. I needed to investigate this house while she slept. There was no way I'd believe her that she had no contact with anyone outside this house.

Something wasn't right here, and I wanted to find out what was going on. I opened the closet, not exactly knowing what to expect, but it was nearly vacant except for a pile of folded linens on a shelf and lone box shoved in a corner, labeled "Library Donations."

A quick glance revealed a pile of books. Maybe I'd find something to read. When I flipped open the lid, feeling a bit guilty for prying into what wasn't my business, I found a handful of mystery thrillers and an old cookbook, none of which appealed to me, so I kept looking. I smiled to myself when I saw an older romance cover I recognized from when I worked at the supermarket in high school. "Bodice rippers," they called them, the hero's shirt opened at the waist, revealing chiseled shoulders and honed abs, the girl's hair floating behind her in the wind. I dug below that pile, and froze.

A black background and a pair of silver handcuffs graced the cover of one, and the handle of a riding crop next to a red rose on the second. I blinked, and knelt in front of the box, closing my eyes at the flood of memories.

Rosalee, tied to the bedpost in the private room where no one would see us. Her head thrown back, eyes closed on the cusp of subspace, her naked form bearing the marks of our session, my power over her, the submission she'd given me willingly, a rare gift...

The month before she left me.

I hadn't taken a sub since.

I shook my head, shoved the books back in the box and pushed the flap down.

I crept out of the room, sure not to make any noise, and I made my way back down to the room I assumed was his office. I tried the door. Locked, as I suspected.

I took a credit card out of my wallet, and kneeling in front of the door, I slid it between the door and strike plate, straightened the card so it was perpendicular to the door, and wriggled until I heard the latch decompress and the lock popped free.

I twisted the knob, my heart tripping in my chest. The door fell open, the darkened interior of his office cold and forbidding. I crept along on the floor, looking around for something that would get me access to the outside world. A computer sat on a large desk in the corner, and to the in front of the desk, two chairs.

I've heard screams.

I've never seen anyone come out of his office.

I groped about the room. I needed a phone. Nothing sat on his desk. He had to have *something.* I yanked open one drawer. Several lengths of rope were neatly tied and stacked in the drawer, bottles of pills, and a sealed black case. I didn't even want to know.

I shut it quickly, opened the second, and froze. A pistol with a silencer sat on the very top but beside the pistol, a cordless phone.

Jesus. Would he have his phone tapped? Did he have surveillance cameras?

After I left this place, I'd never fucking look back.

I stared hard at the door, the image of Rae in my mind.

I lifted the phone, a slim, wireless handset, and felt a surge of relief at the sound of a dial tone. I dialed so quickly, my fingers shook, and I had to re-dial several times before it finally rang.

"Please pick up. Damn it, Seth, pick up the phone."

On the sixth ring, just when I feared it would go to voice-mail, Seth's familiar voice came through on the line. "Hello?"

"Seth. It's me."

A brief pause. "Ryder?" The loud noises in the background nearly drowned out his voice. He had to be at Limits. "Dude, where are you? I almost didn't answer. I don't usually answer private numbers."

"Jesus. I'm stranded in the middle of nowhere. I broke down on Route 249, just outside of Tailborough. I walked like four miles to get to this house and I have no cell reception. Need you to come get me. Now. This place is creeping me the fuck out. Something's not right."

I hissed into the phone as quickly as I could, feeling like someone was watching me from behind but when I turned, I saw nothing but the dark expanse of the hallway behind me. The girl was asleep and the rest of the house was vacant.

"How do I find you?" He asked.

Good fucking question. "Just a minute."

I rifled through the papers on the desk until I found a stack of mail. I matched up the addresses and told him the address.

"I'll get you myself. I'll leave now. For God's sake, be careful."

I hung the phone up, my adrenaline pumping. But as I stood, I remembered the girl who slept upstairs. How could I just leave her like this?

Would she even go if I offered?

Picking up a blank sheet of paper and a pen, I scrawled a quick note. *I had to go. If you ever need anything, call me.*

I scratched my phone number on it and signed it, folded it in three, and wrote RAE across the top, then put everything back just the way it was, looking around me as I did. But I was alone.

I crept back up the carpeted stairs, invigorated now that I knew that help was on its way, my heart slamming against my rib cage. I knelt before Rae's door and slipped the paper underneath. I waited, holding my breath, but no sound came from inside the room. I gave one last look around me before I grabbed my cell phone from the room next to Rae's, shoved it in my pocket, and took off. Tired, hungry, and seriously unsettled, I opened the back door and left.

RAE

I HAD EXPECTED he would leave, but I wasn't sure when. I sat on my bed, listening to the soft sounds of him padding around outside my door, but still I jumped a little when the sliver of white appeared beneath the bottom of the door. I waited a full five minutes, not wanting him to hear me if he was still there, before I unfolded myself from bed and fetched the paper. I sat on the floor and stared at my name written across the top. I closed my eyes briefly. If he had paper and a pen, he'd likely made his way to my father's office, and the only way he'd be able to get in would've been to break in like a burglar.

Maybe my father was right. Maybe people *were* untrustworthy and dangerous. I had almost spent the night under the same roof as a man who was likely a thief, or worse.

I opened the paper, and something inside me warmed. As I sat on the floor with the paper in my hand, I remembered the kindness in his eyes. The way he said my name, and the way he'd touched me when I fell against him. He was strong, and handsome, and he'd proven my father wrong. People weren't all bad.

I wanted to know more about Ryder.

I looked about my room. Where would I hide the paper? Frowning, I scanned my shelves until I found a large, hardcover version of *Robinson Crusoe.* Slipping the book down from the shelf, I tucked the piece of paper in. No one would be the wiser. And it was fitting, putting my note in a book about a shipwrecked man. He'd had no one. Just like me.

With a sigh, I opened the drawer next to my bed and removed the phone I kept hidden in there. My father was the only one who had the number. A pang of guilt plagued me. I'd lied to Ryder and told him I had no phone or way to contact the outside world.

The phone lay silent, though.

I put it back in the drawer. Tonight, I would get some rest and deal with what had happened in the morning.

I WATCHED from my bedroom window as his long, black limousine swung into view. He was four days earlier than expected and I knew why. The only question was, how would he react? I pretended to be reading a book by the window when the door opened and his deep, booming voice called to me from downstairs.

"Rowena!"

For a brief moment, I fantasized about locking the door, pulling out the phone I had for emergencies, and dialing Ryder's number. What would happen then, though? Would I stay behind the closed door and wait for Ryder to come sailing in and somehow miraculously save me? Frankly, I was surprised he'd even left me his number. I mean, I'd whacked him with an iron and not exactly given him the warmest welcome.

"Rowena!" His voice grew louder still, impatient now. "Get down here!"

With a sigh, I put my book down, but not before I removed *Robinson Crusoe* from the shelf and pulled out the paper one last time. I unfolded it and read the number, repeating it to myself. I was sure I wouldn't forget it at this point. I'd recited it to myself hundreds of times a day since he'd left it.

"Yes! I'm here." I walked to the top of the stairs and waved my hand at the furious form of my father on the landing below. "You're early. Welcome home."

"Don't you 'welcome home' me," he said with a glare. "You get down here."

My heart kicked up as I walked down the stairs. What would he do? He never hit me, even when I was a small child. But he had other methods.

"What is it?" I brushed my damp palms against my jeans. "I thought you weren't due home until Friday?"

"It amazes me how easily you lie." The words sank into the pit of my stomach like lead.

I swallowed. "I—I don't know what you mean," I whispered. I stared up at him, and realized that he looked much more tired than I'd seen him in a while. His white hair, shaved short, was thin around the temples, and his ice-blue eyes lined with wrinkles. But even though he was older, now, he still held his body erect, and wielded power.

"I got notification from the surveillance team that there was a trespasser on our property the night before last."

"Oh," I said, waving my hand with an effort to be nonchalant. "Oh, that! Yes, some man's car got stuck on the side of the road, but I'm not sure where. Side of the highway, maybe? But he managed to find his way here and he left shortly after."

"He came in through the *window*. You should have called

the police. But instead of calling the police, you *served him hot chocolate.*"

How did he know everything? My stomach twisted with nausea.

"It seemed the hospitable thing to do."

He shook his head. "Now you see why I have to protect you. Get down here, please."

Slowly I obeyed, though I didn't want to. I wanted to change the subject and pretend this never happened, but I knew he would have his way. He always did. "Sit." He pointed to the chair at the dining room table as he poured himself a drink of Scotch at the sideboard. Once again, it occurred to me that I didn't have to do what he said. I was an adult. I asked myself the same question I had hundreds of times over the past few years.

Why don't you leave?
You don't have to stay.
He doesn't treat you right.

But where would I go? And Ryder's number came to me. I repeated it, as I'd taught myself to do. Up until this point, I knew that if I went anywhere, he would find me. Even the police department was in his pocket. I had no idea what he actually did, but I knew he was powerful, and I knew he was feared.

"Why didn't you tell me right away a man trespassed on our property and entered through your *window?*"

I shrugged. "He seemed harmless."

He slammed his hand on the dining room table so loudly I jumped. "Harmless? He came in the house. He went in my *office.*"

"How do you know that?"

A muscle twitched in his jaw and his eyes narrowed. Not answering the question, he continued his accusations. "He came when no one was here. He could've raped you. He could've taken advantage of you, Rowena!"

"He wouldn't!"

My father's eyes registered first shock, then anger. "Your loyalty lies with a stranger who broke into our home, rather than with the man who rescued you and raised you as his own?"

"Father, I—"

"No. You listen to me. What happened the other night was a danger to you. You've been taught to contact me when anyone comes to the house. You failed me, Rowena, and this must not happen again." He frowned at me, eliciting the familiar feeling of dread disobeying him always caused.

"I didn't mean—"

He picked up his glass and whipped it straight across the room. I screamed. The glass shattering on impact, amber liquid staining the ivory walls. I sat, frozen in place, as he picked up another glass, and another, whipping each one at the wall until a pile of glittering shards lay on the floor of the dining room. "You didn't *mean*," he mocked, a trickle of sweat dripping down from his temple. "You didn't mean *what?* To threaten your safety? To disobey my instructions? To lie to me?"

He stalked closer to me and I shrank into my chair. Though he never raised a hand to me, he didn't have to. His words stung enough.

"I rescued you from poverty, Rowena." His voice softened now as he drew closer and still, I cowered. "I've kept you safe from the evil that surrounds us. I've given you everything you could possibly want, never denied you what you needed."

Everything I needed, except freedom. Friends. Autonomy. Though my contact with the outside world was limited, I knew that people weren't meant to be holed up in houses.

People weren't meant to be isolated and made to feel as if they were useless and stupid.

"I'm sorry, father. It won't happen again," I said.

He sighed heavily and rubbed a hand across his forehead.

"Thank you. Go upstairs for a while. I have some work to do."

I stood, waiting for the other shoe to drop. He wasn't finished with me yet. And as I walked back to my room, his voice arrested me.

"His name, Rowena. Tell me his name."

I swallowed hard. What would he do if he discovered I told a bold-faced lie? "Rhett," I said, reaching for the first name that came to mind, having just finished *Gone with the Wind* the day before. the roguish character's name came out of my mouth

"Rhett."

"Yes. Um, that's what he told me, anyway," I said, not able to look at my father as I told the lie. He stared at me as I left the room and I did my best to ignore him. He would either believe me or he wouldn't.

"Very well," he said, turning away from me.

My stomach in knots, I made my way to the stairs, staring at the doorway that led to the guest room where I'd briefly entertained Ryder. He went to his office, and I started to go to my room, but curiosity got the best of me. He wasn't finished with this, I knew. He wouldn't let this rest until he'd seen Ryder punished.

I waited until I heard him milling about his office, and then I crept downstairs. It was easy to be quiet on the carpeted stairs. I was experienced at it. I used to sneak downstairs to get cookies when it was past my bedtime, or to watch a forbidden TV show after he'd gone to bed. I was only caught a few times, and he always punished me, but it didn't stop me.

I crept down the stairs and slowly made my way to the bathroom that shared a wall with his office. Here, if I removed the grate, I could hear the conversations in his office. I hadn't done it in years.

I shut and locked the door, then scooted over to the vent, knelt down, and lifted out the grate. It fell into my hands easily, as I remembered it would. Leaning up against the wall, my ear at the opening, I could hear my father's voice, distant but clear.

"We had a trespasser in my absence, Russell." Russell was actually Officer Neil Russell, my father's main contact at the police force. "Yes. She won't tell me anything and says she wasn't harmed, but the footage shows the man came into my house *through her bedroom window*. I want you to find out everything you can." He paused. "No, I don't have his name, damn it! And the footage didn't reveal much, because it was so dark out. But I'm sure your men could find details."

Quickly, I replaced the vent, stood, and left the bathroom. My father had set his eyes on Ryder as a target. He was in danger.

I would call him, damn it. I would call him on the only phone I had, and I would find a way to delete his number from the record. I had to. I couldn't stay here one more minute, and I had to warn Ryder that he was in danger. My father would stop at nothing. He would fingerprint his office, whatever pen Ryder used, zoom in with his security cameras on the footage he had. He'd shown me before, proud of how tightly monitored our home was. He didn't harm *me*, but he did have the power to harm others. All he had to do was call the chief of police, and he could do just about anything he wanted.

But even if I could reach Ryder, how would I escape? How would I get away without my father finding out? And when he did, how would I make sure he didn't hurt Ryder? He was a powerful man, and would stop at nothing.

I made my way to my own room, pausing at the doorway as I listened to sounds below. He was still talking on the phone. It was my only chance.

I raced into my room, shut and locked the door. Quickly, I made my decision.

I could not stay here another minute, prisoner from the outside world.

"Are you held here against your own will?" Ryder had asked. Yes, damn it. Yes, I was.

Trembling, I retrieved the phone from the drawer, and dialed the number I'd memorized. My hands shook. What if Ryder didn't answer? I closed my eyes, waiting as the phone rang. My heart soared when I heard his voice.

"Hello, you've reached Ryder."

"Ryder! It's... it's Rae."

"Leave me a message at the beep."

A beep sounded, and I stared at the phone. So it wasn't him after all but his voice mail. I sighed, and at the sound of the beep, I hung up the phone.

Now that I'd called him, I stared at the phone, not sure what to do with it. I'd read some Agatha Christie novels, and knew enough about spying that I suspected something like a tap on the phone, but it had been such a short call. I had to somehow destroy the phone. If my father found out Ryder's number, then all could be lost. But I needed the phone to keep calling. I had to keep trying.

Now, my hand shook as I stared at it. What was more important? Ryder's safety, or my own? My gaze moved to the tall glass of water on the nightstand beside my bed, left over from the night before. All I had to do was drop it in. When I lifted it above the water, though, just an inch or so above the lip of the glass, it lit up and buzzed in my hand.

JANE HENRY

I gasped and sat back on the bed, staring at the phone. I'd never received an incoming call. I hit the green button that flashed in front of me, assuming it meant that was the button that would answer the call and held it up to my ear.

"Hello?" I whispered.

"Hi. I got a call from a number I didn't recognize." Fear and relief wrangled within me. It was Ryder's voice, deep and commanding. He paused, then, "Rae?"

"Yeah?"

"Did you call me?"

I paused and listened. Silence outside my door, which was not good.

I moved as far away from the door as I could, to the large window seat where I read. "Yes," I whispered into the phone. "Can you hear me?"

"Barely. Are you ok?"

"I—I—" The words failed me as my impetuous decision to call him seemed suddenly so stupid.

"Your father is home."

I closed my eyes and nodded, though he couldn't see me.

"Rae?"

"Yes," I whispered. "He's home. I need to leave here, Ryder. I need to get out. And he's trying to track you down. You can't call the police, either. It's too dangerous, because they're his friends."

"What? Jesus. Where are you now?"

"I'm by my window." Still whispering, I tried to talk to him while simultaneously listening for sounds outside my door.

"Did he hurt you?"

How could I answer that question? He never physically hurt me, but every time we spoke, he reminded me of how dependent I was on him, how foolish I was, how I would have to stay here and never leave.

DUNGEON DADDY

"Don't answer," he said. "It'll be safest when it's dark. I'm coming, but I need you to cooperate. Getting out of your window is really tricky because there's nothing to hold on to. Do any of the other windows in your house have an escape route?"

"I have no idea. I don't think so. Oh. Oh, wait! There's a little alcove beneath the guest room. If I could get there, I might be able to get down."

My heart raced as I made plans to leave. I'd never been out of this house, not even once, for as long as I could remember.

"Get to that room. Be ready to leave. Okay?"

"Yes. Thank you."

"Hang up the phone now, and be careful."

"Okay."

We hung up and I stared at the phone and swallowed hard. My hand shook so badly I shoved them in my pockets while I planned my escape. If I left the phone here, he'd find Ryder's number, and if I took it with me, he could possibly track me. It wasn't safe to keep the phone. On impulse, I lifted it above the glass of water, and dropped it in. Water splashed on my dresser, and the phone bobbed up and down crazily. I closed my eyes briefly. It was my only contact to the outside world, and I'd ruined it.

But I was moving on. I didn't need the phone anymore. I had to escape.

Ryder was on his way, and he'd be here soon. What would I take with me? I looked around my room, at the bare walls and spartan-like bed, with its crumpled pink bedspread and stack of pillows. In one corner of the room I had crafts that I occasionally worked on, needlework, watercolors, and beading. None of it mattered. It would all be reminiscent of a life held captive.

I squared my shoulders and walked to my door, needing

to get to the guest room and scope out the escape route. But when I tried the doorknob, to my shock, I found it locked. I twisted it again, and but it didn't budge. I closed my eyes, willing the door to open, but knowing it would not.

I fell to the floor and sat heavily, tucking my legs underneath me, closing my eyes.

There was no way he already knew that I was leaving.

This was my punishment for my lie.

RYDER

Jesus. The girl called me. I didn't know her at all, and had no idea what I would do with her, but I couldn't leave her locked up in that house against her will. I was getting in deep, and I knew it, the second she said, "Don't call the police."

God. What would I do with her?

The safest place for her would be at Limits, with me, where I employed a team of bodyguards and security, and every connection I had was within arm's reach. But how did a girl who knew nothing about the outside world fit in at a club like mine?

I shoved my phone in my pocket, frowning at the black door to my office and thought for a few minutes, but I didn't have much time to think. I had to activate my men, and I had to do it now. As owner of the most exclusive nightclub on the east coast, I had serious responsibilities, but the plus side was, I had a team that worked for me that I could depend on.

But once I took the girl and brought her here, there would be no getting out of this mess, and there was no denying the fact that the man she called "father," the one who held her hostage, was a dangerous person.

Walking across my office, I opened the door and scanned the interior of Limits. Immediately, the gazes of the occupants inside came to me, but there were only three I cared about: Dean, Seth, and Caden, the men on the floor tonight. I needed muscle and speed, and they were the men for the job. I lifted my hand and all but Caden. the bouncer at the door, came to me. I gave him a nod, showing him that I recognized he couldn't leave and circled my finger around the floor, then tapped the speaker at my ear.

"Yeah, boss?"

"Need a meeting with everyone. I need to leave, and I need some assistance. How many do you need here on staff?"

He scanned the crowd. "We have two hundred and fifty strong here, four stationed upstairs and four downstairs. Leave me one more on the main, and I'm good."

"You've got it," I said, and saluted him with one finger across the room. He saluted back. Tonight was a slow night, but would slowly pick up as it got closer to the weekend, Thursday gaining momentum, Friday doubling our Wednesday night guests, and then Saturday we'd peak at maximum capacity.

Clients of Limits were the richest, most powerful people in America, and we were the East Coast's most exclusive Club. Members had to apply for admission, and we went through a rigorous screening process. I didn't fuck around when it came to safety. Dean and Seth were tough and rugged, Seth a jiu jitsu master with a black belt. They'd both watch my back. I opened the door to my office and gestured for them to come in, then tapped the earpiece that would allow me to speak to the entire staff.

"All staff on alert. I've had a serious personal matter come up that needs my immediate attention. I'm taking Dean and Seth with me, and leaving Caden as Master in Charge in my absence. Go to him with any issues."

Murmured responses of "Yes, sir," and "Got it, boss," came to me before I clicked it off.

These men and women were my brothers and sisters, and I trusted them with my life. I'd handpicked my staff. They were trustworthy and professional and would take care of shit while I was gone.

The door clicked shut and I tossed my earpiece on my desk, reached for my tie and loosened it.

"We gotta be quick, guys. we need to move now. I'll explain on the way."

Seth, a tall, muscular guy with swarthy skin, eyed me with his coal-black gaze, his clean-shaven jaw tight. His eyes glittered, already on alert for the details. He knew if I pulled him and Dean off the floor, it was for good reason. I knew no other Dominant as self-possessed as Seth, and no other who could knock skulls together as effectively either if necessary.

Dean was the badass of the group, having served time in his younger years but reformed behind bars, lifting weights and channeling his need for control into pursuing the BDSM lifestyle. He had a regular submissive of over twelve years, and didn't play on the side, but worked full-time for me. I'd never even met his wife, but knew she was a Harvard professor and department chair in one of the sciences. He didn't offer information and I didn't ask questions.

"What's up, Chief?" Dean asked, leaning against the bookshelf.

"The other night, I broke down on Route 249, off the main drag down in a remote area of Tailborough." I nodded to Seth. "Blew a tire, and tried to call for help but was in a dead zone, and couldn't reach anyone." Dean's typically jovial eyes sobered. "Found a house, got no answer, even though lights were on and I saw a shadow in the window. A woman's."

JANE HENRY

Dean's brow rose and Seth pushed away from the wall, but neither spoke.

Dean's lip curled, but I ignored him.

"I looked up and tried to get her attention, but the next thing I knew, she screamed and fell, and from where I stood, it looked like someone had pulled her from behind. I yelled, got no answer, so I climbed up to see if she needed help."

"You climbed up?" Seth's deep, midnight voice boomed across the room. I swallowed.

"Yeah. Climbed up."

"A random house in the middle of nowhere, that looked like it was *intended* to be in the middle of nowhere. And you scaled the fucking siding."

"Sure as hell did, Seth, now shut up and listen."

His eyes narrowed but he didn't say anything else while I continued.

"Here's the bottom line, guys. There was a woman in that room. She's a captive in that house. Her father won't allow her access to the outside world. No internet. No leaving the house. no contact with anyone besides him."

"Jesus," Seth muttered.

"No shit," Dean agreed.

"But she didn't want to hear anything about leaving. Creepy as fuck. So I waited until she was asleep, broke into her father's office, and that's when I got in touch with Seth, who agreed to pick me up, and I went back to my car." I cleared my throat. "Left my number for the girl, slipped it under her door. Tonight, she called me. Her father's home, and he knows I was there."

Dean whistled but Seth just stared.

"She want out?" Dean asked.

"Yep."

"So there's a psycho chick you barely met—"

"She's not a psycho, asshole."

Dean blinked, then nodded. "Okay so there's this... girl—I mean, woman—held captive. And her psycho father won't let her leave the house, and you one day out of the blue wander in like her fucking Prince Charming to which she's all *'oh, only guy I've ever met in my life, let me call him and is risking his life so he can rescue me.'*"

"Shut it," Seth ordered, his narrowed eyes swinging around to Dean. "This is what I hear. Captive girl held against her will by a sick fucker, asking for help to escape. I have only one question."

"Yeah?"

"Why haven't we left yet?"

WE PARKED the car a good distance away from the house, but needed to move.

"What do you know about her father?" Seth grilled me as I drove.

"Once I left that place I didn't want to remember a fucking thing."

"Except the girl," Dean said.

I shot Dean a glare. Yeah, I remembered the girl all right. I'd checked my phone every hour since I'd left. I remembered her wide brown eyes, saucy mouth, and curves. The fetching way her cheeks turned pink when I told her I'd spank her. I'd replayed that memory many times.

"Here. I'm parking here." I figured at this point I was as close to the house as I could get without being noticed, but I needed to move fast. "I told her to meet me in the room next to hers. And I want to be sure we get to that side, first."

"It isn't the room where you scaled the wall to get to her?" Dean asked.

"No, it's too damn hard to get to."

Seth nodded. "Go. You go get her, I'll keep an eye here."

"Perfect. Dean, you get in the driver's seat. I want you ready to take off the second I've got her, okay?"

He grinned. He'd been dying to get behind the wheel of my car.

"Hell yeah."

I crouched close to the ground and ran, Seth at my side.

I shook my head. I would I'd get her. What I would do when I got her I had no idea, but that wasn't the most important thing now. I finally made it to where she should be and scanned the quickest way to get to her, when something hit the ground several yards away on the other side of the house. I froze.

"What was that?" I hissed to Seth, but he was already on his way over to investigate.

"What the fuck?" He muttered. "It's a dead cell phone."

"What?"

He showed it to me, then, an ancient cell phone with water dripping from it, half broken now.

"Where did it come from?" If her father was the one who threw it out… damn it. What if we were too late?

I drew closer to the house and moved as quickly and as stealthily as I could to the other side where the cell phone had fallen, hoping I could get a glimpse into one of the windows, but it was so dark out, and I didn't dare risk shining a flashlight. Seth was at my back, when another *smack* hit the ground. I squinted in the inky blackness. What had fallen? I got on all fours and crawled toward where I'd heard the sound, and my hand hit the hard edge of a book. I picked it up, but couldn't see anything. I held it up silently to Seth, when another *smack* hit right next to me.

"She's tossing stuff from her window, or someone is," I said, holding up another book, and craning my neck. And

DUNGEON DADDY

then the clouds shifted, moonlight filtering through, and I saw her, her long honey-colored hair floating around her, as she waved her hand frantically, but didn't make a sound.

What the fuck was she doing in her room? I'd told her to leave. I glared in the darkness and mouthed *what are you doing there?* But of course, she didn't see me.

"She's in her room," I hissed. "I have to get up there."

"Jesus."

"Keep an eye out."

I groaned. It had been hard enough the first time getting up there.

I had no choice though.

I launched myself to the first level alcove hanging beside the house as I'd done before. I dragged myself up to the flower box and pulled myself up, shimmying to the ledge.

I finally got to the balcony. The door was wide open when I got there, and she grabbed me, pulling me into the room. Unsteady, I crashed onto the floor.

"Rae," I groaned. She tried to help me up, but I shrugged her off, glaring. "*Why* didn't you go where I told you to go?"

She shook her head. "He locked me in," she whispered, and then froze. Her eyes widened as we heard a door slamming below. She knelt in front of me and exhaled. "Phew. That means he's going into his office, and he won't come out for hours."

"Hours? He locked you in your room with no way out? What if you have to use the bathroom?"

She pointed to a door I hadn't seen before. "I have my own bathroom," she whispered. "It's tiny, but it works."

"Why'd he lock you in here?" I asked, then shook my head. "Know what? I don't want to know. I've got a man in a car ready to take you out of here and someone watching below. He'll flash a light if there's danger." I paused and I couldn't help it then, my instincts to protect this girl taking over. I grabbed her by the chin and gave her my sternest look, making sure she looked me in the eyes. "Are you *sure* this is what you want to do? Because we could get in serious trouble here. You know that, right?"

She held my large hands in her small ones, as she stared at me. "I know. I need to leave here, Ryder. I need to get *out.*"

That was all I needed to know. With one quick nod, I pulled her to stand and led her with one hand gripping hers, to the bathroom. "Let me scope this out. There's no way we can safely get out through your bedroom window. Getting up is hard enough. But if we can get out the bathroom…"

I peeked out the window, but below the window lay nothing but a wide, vast expanse. Jesus. We couldn't go out that way either.

"We're gonna have to break out of your room and risk leaving another way," I said.

"Oh, God." Her voice shook and she held my hand tighter.

"There's nothing to be afraid of. One old man isn't gonna be able to take on three grown men and a headstrong woman, right?"

"You don't know him," she said, shaking her head, but I pulled her along to the door.

"Don't need to."

I tried the lock first. To my shock, the knob twisted, and with a little click, the door fell open. I turned in surprise to Rae, who only shook her head in shock, her mouth dropping open.

"I—I swear to you it was locked a short while ago," she whispered. "He must've decided it was long enough."

I gestured for her to get behind me as I tentatively peeked around the edge of the door, prepared to defend her if anyone threatened her safety, but the hallway was vacant. We moved quickly through the hallway and down the stairs, still holding hands. Eventually, he'd see that she was gone, but our getaway would be easier if we were uninhibited, so the point now was to get out safely and quickly. She followed behind me in silence, until we got to the landing at the bottom of the stairs.

At the door, she froze. "I don't know. Ryder, I don't know. Once I leave, there's no coming back."

I looked at her in surprise. She was a brave, headstrong woman, but now she looked like a little child, her eyes wide and fearful, her lower lip trembling. I wanted to pull her to me and kiss her, tuck her against my chest and tell her everything would be alright.

"There's no turning back," I told her. "You're right. But if you stay here, Rae? There's no going forward, either."

She blinked, then briefly closed her eyes, nodded her head, and followed me out to the cool, dark night, where Seth and Dean waited for us. I expected some sort of flashing lights or sirens to go off, as if we'd just robbed a bank but there was nothing. No reaction, nothing at all but the crunch of leaves and twigs underfoot and our heavy breathing as we panted from exertion.

Once we were at the car, I hastily buckled Rae's belt for her, ignoring her protests, then sidled in on the other side.

"Go!"

We peeled off and I listened for the sounds of pursuit behind us, but all I heard was her muffled cries.

"No one's coming," Dean said, as I continued to look out the window, making sure we weren't followed. It wouldn't be safe to bring her to Limits if anyone knew we were there, but if we made our escape unnoticed then it would be the safest place around, as we were heavily guarded with staff that was trained to defend.

I directed Dean to bring us the back way, so we could

enter through the employee entrance and hopefully avoid as much notice as possible. Rae sat quietly next to me.

"No one followed us?" she asked.

"No. Looks like we're fine. For now," I added. I couldn't shake the eerie feeling that we *hadn't* just snuck the man's prized possession from his property without notice. We'd see retaliation, I had no doubt, but for now she was safe.

CHAPTER 5

Rae

I couldn't seem to grasp what was happening to me. Would I wake up and find this was all a dream? Had it really been that easy to escape my cage? I looked at my surroundings, and tried to figure out where we were. Ryder and two seriously scary-looking guys had taken me to this gigantic building that looked like it belonged in some sort of exclusive magazine for rich people or something. Sparkling chandeliers decorated the inside of the place, breathtaking artwork in splashes of black and silver scattered on the walls, thick carpets lining the lounge areas with plush, comfortable-looking couches and chairs. And there were people everywhere, dressed up in formal blacks and grays, holding long-stemmed glasses and frothy steins.

He ushered me into an office and shut the door.

"Where are we?"

"Limits." His voice was as I remembered, deep and commanding. I felt somehow calmer just listening to him speak. "It's a high-end club I own and manage. Exclusive membership, heavy security." He walked over to his desk and leaned against the edge, shoving his hands in his pockets. He wore black slacks and a white t-shirt that stretched across the large expanse of his chest. A scruffy beard covered his strong jaw, and his bright blue eyes narrowed in on me. I shivered a bit. I couldn't believe I'd whacked this man upside the head with an iron. He could be very intimidating.

"I—I... um... can't believe I knocked you out," I said, grimacing. "And you still came and rescued me."

There was no humor in his gaze as he stared at me, his large arms folded across his chest sternly. "I can't believe you did either," he said. "Though in your defense, you thought I was a burglar." He frowned but his eyes twinkled just the tiniest bit. "You try something like that *here*, though, and I'll turn you over my knee. Before, we were on your turf. Now, we're on mine. Got it?"

I blinked and wondered if I'd heard him correctly. My cheeks flamed, and I wasn't exactly sure why. "Excuse me?"

"Listen, Rae. I just risked serious danger to myself and my crew by coming to get you. Now, I did it because I wanted to. Freaks me the fuck out to think of you being held in that house like a prisoner. And no one should ever have to do anything against their will. But you're *here*, now. And the moment you called me, you made me your protector. You get that?"

No. No, I didn't get that. But what had I expected?

"I didn't ask you to be my protector."

"Yeah you did. You asked me to rescue you, and put my personal safety, and the safety of those who work for me, at risk. So now, we do things on my terms."

Part of me felt anger flare up at the audacity, but he also had a point. It wasn't like I could offer to pay him or anything.

"Ok. And those terms are…"

"First, you and I have a talk." He walked over to me and as he grew closer, my heart kicked up. Why was he coming over to me? But then he walked right past me to the door to his office, and snapped the lock. "Just so we have some privacy," he said.

"So here we are." He pulled a chair over and put it right next to me, so close I could smell his cologne, pine and musk and mint. Being this close to him I could see the little hairs under his shirt peeking out, see the well-defined muscles of his shoulders and abs, and my body began to respond. I swallowed and ran my tongue over my dry lips.

"Yes?"

His eyes held mine. "Full disclosure. I run a high-end club for people with particular tastes. I was an investor for years before I bought this club."

My heart raced even more, and my mouth grew dry, but I tried to keep my reactions under wraps. "Oh?"

He kept right on as if I hadn't said anything at all. "This is not only the place I run, but my home."

Wowww. He lived at this swanky place? It made the house I lived in look like a dollhouse. This place was amazing. I'd never been out of my house, but I'd read plenty. I knew there were apartments in urban areas, and large country houses, and tiny, run-down places in inner cities, among other things. And I knew enough to know this was a place for people who were very, *very* well off.

"Tell me everything you know about your father."

I didn't expect him to ask that, so I dropped my head and my words became hushed. "What do you want to know?"

"What does he do for work? What sort of man is he? How did he get *you*?"

I shook my head, feeling like an idiot, for I knew hardly

any of the answers to his questions. "Well," I cleared my throat. "I know he gives loans to people."

Ryder's eyes narrowed.

"He... says that I'm very special to him. That he loves me." No reaction. "But as I've told you before, he says the outside world is a scary place to be, and he prefers to protect me from dangerous elements that could harm me."

Still, no reaction.

"As far as how I came to live with him, I have no idea. He says I'm his daughter." I paused. "But I know that isn't true."

Ryder cocked his head to the side, and still said nothing, just waited for me to explain. There was something about his stern eyes, the way his jaw clenched and his brows drew together, that made me quiver. I didn't know why. I wasn't afraid of him. But deep down inside, I knew he was a man that *could* be quite fearful... not the way my father was. But there was something serious about his demeanor that I couldn't quite reconcile.

I reached for a lock of my hair and twisted it around my finger, the light reflecting on the shining gold. "I know I'm not his, because of something one of his staff said once. I was supposed to be in bed one night, but I'd forgotten my book down in the dining room. I went to get it but was quiet about it, because if I got out of bed past my bedtime, he would punish me. The door to his office was opened, and I overheard one of his associates saying that my parents had been found dead. They'd frozen to death somewhere, I don't know where, but their bodies were found. I guess he'd been keeping tabs on them. And that's all I know."

I felt better having told him this, though my voice shook and I felt strangely as if I needed to cry. I hadn't spoken to more than a handful of people in my entire life—only the man I called father, and the occasional staff members he'd employed over the years. But he never kept anyone long enough for me to get to really know them.

I didn't know I was crying until a tear splashed onto my cheek. I wiped it hastily away, but it was too late. Ryder had seen it. He took my hand in his much larger one, his fingers twice the size of mine, lightly covered in dark hair, warm and reassuring. He squeezed, and my body responded. It shocked me how warmth flooded my body, my belly clenching, my breasts swelling. At his touch, the lump in my throat dissolved, and I cried in earnest, the entire situation so difficult for me to grasp. I'd left the only home I'd ever known, a place where I'd been held against my will. I'd been lied to and manipulated. But now I didn't know what was up or down, or who to trust.

"C'mere," Ryder said gruffly, opening his arms and gesturing for me to come near. I hesitated at first, but the next thing I knew he'd pulled me bodily into his arms and smoothed a hand over the back of my head, encouraging me to rest my head on his shoulder.

"This has been a really hard night for you," he said softly. I couldn't believe so big and stern could be so gentle, but it seemed I'd drawn it out of him.

"It has," I sniffled.

"I bet you're confused, and scared, and a whole bunch of other things at once, aren't you?" he asked, his deep voice soft.

I nodded, the tears flowing harder at his sympathetic tone.

"This is what we're going to do. We have some serious decisions to make, Rae. Do you want to stay here with me? And avoid detection from the man you lived with?"

That was an easy decision to make. I nodded.

"You can't walk around the way you look now, recognizable by anyone who could be looking for you. Do you understand that?" I nodded my head. He was right. I'd have to change the way I looked and dress.

"Yes," I sniffled. "You're right. I do."

He ran his hand through my long, thick hair, and sighed. "Your hair is beautiful. Absolutely stunning. But so is the rest of you."

I warmed at that, and drew a little closer. "Thank you," I whispered.

"Tonight, I'll bring you up to my room. Tomorrow, I'll get some contacts I know together to come up with a way to protect your identity. Okay?"

I nodded. "Yes."

"You're tired and you need some sleep. Let's go upstairs now." He released me, gently pushing me to my feet, then stood, taking my hand.

"If I make it known you're mine, no one here will come near you. So from now on, you're mine. Got it?"

Hope flared in my chest, and a strange sort of excitement stirred within me. "Yours," I repeated. "I pretend to be yours. Yes. Yes, I can do that."

He smiled, his eyes warming me, and I felt the rush of heat and excitement again. "Good girl."

I liked that. He opened the door to his office and at once the bright lights and sounds accosted me. I'd never seen anything like this, and it was all I could do not to throw my hands up to block out the lights, or cover my ears to stop the sound. Its relentlessness was overwhelming.

"Focus on me, Rae," he said. "Just follow me."

A huge guy with a shaved head and the biggest muscles I'd ever seen approached us and said something to Ryder, but I couldn't hear. "Yeah," Ryder replied. "Watch the feed closely and if you see anything out of place, you come immediately to me. No screwing around. You get me?"

"Yes, sir," the big guy said, and he left.

Wow. Ryder was in charge here. I liked that.

"It's loud in here," I said, screwing my face up against the noise. I felt physically ill with the pulsating music and couples nearby. Ryder looked at me for a moment, his dark eyes serious and probing, before he took my hand.

"I imagine you haven't had much of a chance to get out. Loud crowds unfamiliar to you?"

I nodded. "You could say that."

But as we walked hand in hand, it felt a bit easier to bear.

"This way, Rae," he said, tugging my hand to the right of the large dance floor. People danced in one area, with a crystal globe thing spinning above the floor, casting flashes of brilliant light below it, and a large bar looped in a corner, the ceiling dotted with a million white lights that looked like stars in the night sky. Brilliant blue illuminated the seats below the bar, giving the entire area a sort of otherworldly glow. It was magical, if a bit intimidating. Three bartenders worked the bar, their hands moving quickly and efficiently, as frothy glasses of beer and delicate long-stemmed glasses of wine passed hands. To the right of the bar was what looked like a lounge area, with black leather couches and pillows, couples comfortably sitting and chatting. It seemed like what I'd imagine a typical nightclub would look like, but there was an undercurrent I couldn't quite put my finger on. Not having ever experienced anything like this before, I didn't know how to identify it.

Ryder leaned in and whispered in my ear. "My room is upstairs. Once we get up there we'll have some quiet." His breath warmed my cheek, and I shivered against him. I was glad he'd made me pretend to be his. Without him at my side, I felt completely exposed.

We passed the people in the lounge area and came to a narrow hall. Though I'd only gotten a glimpse into a small part of Limits, I could tell that it was enormous, several stories big. We made our way toward a large set of silver elevator doors in the hallway. I was thankful I'd read a lot of books and had and watched enough TV that none of this was completely foreign to me. I'd just never experienced any of it before.

A beep sounded nearby that made me jump, but Ryder merely took his phone out of his pocket without breaking stride, still holding my hand. He tapped a button on the phone, then shut it off and pushed something by his ear. It took me a moment to realize he'd transferred the call from his phone to his earpiece. "Use channel A," he ordered. "We're back and I won't be leaving again tonight."

He nodded and "mmhmm'd" a bit, but didn't say anything else for a moment. He stopped in front of the elevator, pointed for me to stay right where I was, and smacked a round button with an up-arrow. I watched in fascination as the arrow lit up and the numbers above the door indicated floor the elevator was on. There were three floors in total. The elevator stopped at one, and the large doors opened, revealing a glass interior, a mirrored ceiling, and a silver bar to hold onto. Ryder gently shoved me on.

"Go on. Hit the button for the third floor." I did what he asked, as he finished his call.

"No signs we were followed? Good. Yes. Have Dean activate the second level of surveillance. Yes, that one. We haven't used it in four years, haven't needed to, but I want it on tonight and until further notice. Be sure all staff knows Caden is Master in Charge on the main floor, Dean surveys all play on the second floor, and you're to report to me with *anything* suspicious, and I mean *anything*. And have some rumors spread that I have..." He paused and looked at me. "That I have a new submissive."

Oh.

I kept my mouth closed, not knowing how to respond.

He hung up the phone, and the doors to the elevator opened.

He'd called me his submissive. He wanted them to believe that's who I was.

I didn't know how I felt about that.

Had he found my books? Did he know I liked to read… those kinds of romance books? It had all started with a box of books our housecleaner had gotten from the library book drive. She'd felt badly for me, being all alone, and brought them one day when my father was traveling. She didn't speak much English and said something about these being free, to just take out what I liked.

I'd gone through until I found some with covers that intrigued me. Not knowing what I was getting into, I started reading one night, and was pulled in to a world I never knew existed. It was certainly nothing I'd ever read in any of the classics father provided me with.

He led me down the hallway in silence, his shoes clicking softly on the beautiful ivory and gold floor. I expected he'd take out a key when we arrived at the large black doorway, but he merely flicked a button, tapped a few numbers into a keypad, and the door slid open.

"How'd you do that?"

"Keyless entry, programmed to recognize me."

"So no one else could get into your place without you being there?"

"Exactly."

Now that we were so close to being alone, my heart kicked up again. I wasn't sure how I felt being in a place that no one could access but him. Had I gone from one prison to another?

The door clicked shut behind me. He walked past me, and I stood, frozen in place, not sure if I was supposed to follow him or stay where I was. He flicked a light on, illuminating the room, and I caught a brief glimpse of an immaculate kitchen to the left, cast in shadow, and in front of me a large living room area with a fireplace that flanked one wall. Huge, comfortable-looking mahogany couches, gleaming hardwood floors, and the best part of all, a bookshelf laden with books of every shape and size.

I jumped at the sound of Ryder's deep, commanding voice from the living room. "Rae, come in here."

Walking toward him, I felt a bit shy, but I was also both exhausted and exhilarated. I froze when I reached the living room. Ryder sat in one of the big chairs. He leaned over, untying his shoelaces and there was something about the intimacy of the moment that intimidated me. He paused, one hand on a lace, and lifted his eyes to me. "I said come here." There was no humor in his gaze now, as he looked at me across the room. He wasn't quite... angry. But he wasn't pleased. "Why are you standing there?"

I blinked and didn't move. He sat up then, frowning. "Listen, Rae, I'm taking it easy on you, knowing you came from... a difficult past. But you need to know that I'm not the kind of guy that likes being disobeyed."

Disobeyed?

My heart fluttered madly as I walked closer to him somehow, not understanding why I was suddenly so paralyzed with fear, but knowing that I didn't like Ryder displeased with me.

"You said to pretend I was your submissive. What does that mean?" I blurted out, sitting heavily on the edge of the couch furthest from him. I didn't know how he'd react, but his grin surprised me.

"You heard that, huh?"

Heard it? You could say that.

"What is a submissive, Ryder? What does that *mean?*" I had a vague notion but needed to hear it from him.

He sat back, and the humor fled his face. Folding his arms across his chest, he looked at me. "Do you understand that if you're honest with me, things will be much better between us? I understand that you may have learned to hide the truth as a sort of defense mechanism, and I get that. But I want you to stop lying to me now."

My cheeks enflamed, and I looked away quickly, literally squirming in my seat. I felt naked, as if a spotlight shone on me in a crowded room, and I wanted to hide. "I don't know what you're talking about," I said in a rush.

"Stop."

The sharpness of his tone made me jump. I blinked, then lifted my gaze to his. His eyes met mine, serious and stern, but his voice was softer now. "Rae, *stop*. You came to me for help. Now you need to trust me. And the first rule I have is that you have to be honest with me. No lying. Do you understand?"

I nodded my head and swallowed, grateful he didn't ask me to speak for I didn't trust my voice.

He leaned forward, his forearms resting on his knees, his blue eyes meeting mine without blinking. "I found a box of books at your house. Tell me the truth. Were they yours?"

I swallowed. "Yes."

"Did you read them?"

I looked away but his sharp rebuke pulled me back. "Look at me."

I obeyed. "Yes. Yes, I did."

"And you sit here and ask me what a submissive is?" He raised a brow at me. He knew that though I was kept apart from the world, I did in fact know what he referred to.

"I want to hear how *you* define a submissive."

His eyes narrowed and a muscle twitched in his jaw. "What do you think it is?"

Fine, then. He wanted me to tell him what I thought? "A

submissive is *not* weak," I said. "They willingly give their trust to a Dominant partner. Someone who has some measure of authority over them. The different ways Dominants and submissives interact varies greatly. Sometimes there is a total power exchange, and the dominant partner controls every interaction they have, every part of his or her submissive's day, from the clothes they wear to the food they eat. And sometimes, it's just a matter of play, and couples even switch roles. But the crux of it all is trust, no matter the level of power exchange, and the submissive who gives him or herself willingly to someone in authority over them reaps the freedom of a quiet mind."

I finished speaking, and felt my cheeks burn.

I had *not* meant to say all that.

His eyes were wider than before, perhaps in surprise. "That's a very thorough answer, and a good start," he said. "So yes. I'm a Dominant. The exchange varies greatly, but I like having as much control as my submissive will give me."

Something about the way he said *my submissive* warmed me through, but I couldn't look away this time. "I've asked you for total honesty so I will give that back to *you* now." He sat back, and clasped his hands behind his head. "I've been a dominant since I knew that my need for control was acceptable in certain circles. That's going on two decades now. I've had a variety of submissives, but I've not had one for over a year. My last partner met a man at this club, and got pregnant with his baby before I even realized she was cheating on me."

"Oh, my," I breathed. "That's terrible."

He nodded. "It was. It stung and that's putting it mildly. I haven't taken a submissive since." He looked over my shoulder then, as if lost in his own thoughts. "I run this club. I live here. It's an easy alibi, saying you're my submissive, because people here expect me to take one. They'll be happy for me. They'll be good to you. And I can keep you under wraps pretty easily."

I shivered a little but hid it with a shrug. I swallowed. "So what does... being a Dominant mean to *you?*"

His gaze came back to mine, and he sobered. "I like total control, Rae. But I only take as much as my submissive will give me. Control freely given is a gift. I would never want it any other way." It seemed like an odd conversation to have, sitting in the room of a man I hardly knew, who'd taken me out of the only home I'd ever known at my request. Worried that my father would pursue me, and unsure of what I'd do with myself *tonight,* never mind the rest of my life.

"Yeah. Yeah, that makes sense," I said. "So what are you like... as a Dominant?" I tried to surreptitiously wipe my damp palms on my thighs, swallowing though my mouth was dry. I couldn't quite look at him while I waited for his answer. I liked the idea of being cared for as a submissive, to be the utter focus of someone's attention.

"What am I like as a Dominant?" he asked, tipping his head to the side. "I think you'll find out soon enough. For now, it's time to get you to bed. You'll be sleeping in here with me, so I can keep you safe and make sure that we don't arouse any suspicion. Understood?"

I nodded, and suddenly the mere suggestion of rest made my eyes feel heavy. It had been such a long day, a day that seemed like it had lasted far longer than twenty-four hours.

He stood then, and I was reminded of how tall he was. "So this is my main living area. I like things simple in my private quarters, as I spend most of my time down in Limits. You know?" I nodded. No, I didn't know, but I could hazard a guess or two. "So here is the kitchen," he waved his hand in the general direction of the kitchen. "I have a few stools against the counter in the kitchen, and I typically eat there. Really there are only two rooms in this place. This one here, that you've already seen," and he pointed to where we were sitting a moment ago. "And the bedroom."

My tummy dipped, but he continued. "Tonight, I'll sleep on the couch and you'll take my bed." He didn't ask or even hint, but instructed me, so I followed, not knowing how to respond. I didn't want him sleeping on the couch, but I also knew by now that Ryder expected me to do as I was told. He led me past the couch, to where a doorway lay hidden in the shadows. I hadn't seen it before, and now I felt my heartbeat racing as we came near. My hands shook, my mouth dry. It was only a bedroom. Why was I reacting this way?

He turned the knob, and the door opened. He flicked on a light, walked in the room, and beckoned for me to come in. A huge, four-poster bed stood in the center of the room, covered in a black quilt. A pile of fluffy white pillows lay at the head of the bed, and at the foot of the bed sat a mahogany chest. There was a glass-topped table to the right of the bed, and a small black basket with coins, next to a sleek black charging station. On the left side of the room sat a small desk with a chair, and above that a small shelf housed a few hardcover books—I eyed a John Grisham, Steven King, and some business titles I didn't recognize. Above the bed hung a framed print, black and white bare tree branches against a cloudless sky. He opened a closet, and removed some blankets. "Extra blankets if you need them. I'll give you some of my clothes to sleep in. Tomorrow, we'll take care of the rest."

"This is like some weird sort of sleepover," I said, before I realized what I was saying. He paused, his hand frozen on the doorknob to the bathroom and turned to me, his lips quirking up.

"Yeah," he said with a huff of laughter. "I'm not sure you're ready to play truth or dare with me."

My cheeks flushed and I looked away, but his voice called my attention back to him.

"Hey, I'm teasing. So let's get you what you need, okay?" His voice had gentled considerably. I only nodded. So much was on my mind. So much troubled me. But listening to his calm reassurance gave me a little bit of hope.

He walked over to a tall dresser that stood in the corner of the room, and removed a t-shirt and a pair of boxers. "Here. Get changed into these, and I'll have your clothes cleaned for the morning."

I nodded. "Thank you, Ryder."

"You're very welcome. Now get some rest."

He left the room. I stared at the door for a moment before I picked up the clothes and stripped out of my jeans and top, neatly folding them into a pile and laying them on the chair beside the desk. The entire room was so masculine, I felt a bit like an imposter.

Who was I kidding? I *was* an imposter. I didn't belong here. But I didn't belong where I'd been kept for my whole life either. The very thought of returning to the dismal, heartless home where I'd been raised depressed me.

I prepared for bed, sliding into his t-shirt, but the boxers were so big they wouldn't stay up. I tossed them to the side and climbed under the covers, my eyes heavy as I tried to stop my brain, hoping that rest would come. I hated that the door was closed. It made me feel like I did at home, closed off from everyone and everything around me. I scooted out of bed and opened the door.

"Ryder?" A few seconds later, I heard him approaching. Oh, God. He'd stripped to just his boxers, and stood in front of me bare-chested, hair tousled. His huge shoulders dwarfed the door frame, as he leaned against it. A smattering of dark hair covered his chest, tapering down his hardened abs to his boxers. I breathed in deep and breathed out, my body awash with a hum of excitement.

"Yeah?" His gaze roamed over my body before he quickly

looked me in the eyes, but I watched as his Adam's apple bobbed up and down when he swallowed. "You need something?"

"I can't sleep with the door closed."

He blinked then shrugged. "Okay. Well, then, leave it open."

"You don't mind?"

"Of course, I don't mind. Now go to bed, Rae." He pointed back to the bed and shot me a stern look. I scooted over, lifted the covers, and slid underneath. He padded back to the couch.

"Ryder?" I yelled out, even though he was now on his couch away from the door.

"Yeah?" he yelled back.

"Thank you!"

"You're welcome. Now go to sleep!"

"Okay, okay." I laid there, but sleep would not come.

CHAPTER 6

Ryder

I LISTENED for the sounds of her resting, but all I heard was her tossing and turning. If this girl were anyone else, I'd have threatened to warm her ass if she didn't settle down, but I still wasn't sure what I could expect from her. I grabbed my phone to check in with Dean and Seth, but all was quiet. No one had spotted a disturbance, nothing was out of the ordinary. My gut said something was off, though. Something wasn't right, but for now, the girl was safe.

Tomorrow, I'd pull together a team to make sure no one hurt her, and do a full investigation into the man she called father. I had a lot of work to do, but fortunately enough the people who worked for me would make the task much easier. My eyes were heavy and I wanted to sleep, but I couldn't, not yet, not until I knew that she'd fallen asleep.

What had that man done to her? She said he never touched her, and I'd have to take her word for it. But what other damage had he inflicted? The eyes that met mine were brave, intelligent, and inquisitive, but I couldn't help but wonder what lurked behind them.?

I knew the demons I fought, and I battled them daily.

What were hers?

I shut my eyes and had just begun to drift to sleep when I heard the floor creaking behind me. I clenched my teeth and sat up, opening my eyes with considerable effort as I looked over at her, standing in the doorway to the living room.

"Rae, you need to get some sleep, and I do, too. Why the hell are you out of bed again, and what do you need from me?"

I would not look at the nipples that poked the t-shirt. Nope. I wasn't going to gape at her full breasts that would stretch my shirt beyond repair, or the way the clingy fabric hugged her sweet curves. I cleared my throat and willed my cock to stop fucking with my head.

"Do you mind if I read one of your books?" she asked. "I can't sleep."

I exhaled, my patience waning. "You woke me up so that you could ask me if you could read my books? Yeah. For fuck's sake, read the books. Use my iPad. I don't care what you do, just be quiet so I can get some rest."

Her eyes flashed at my tone. "You don't have to be a jerk about it." She crossed her arms and glared at me.

Is that how it was going to be? I swung my legs over the side of the couch and pushed myself to standing. To her credit, she didn't back down, but marched over to me, pointing a finger in my direction. "I've spent my entire life having to ask permission for everything. So *excuse me* if I have a hard time shaking it. Okay? God!"

"Whoa, now, woman," I said, shaking my head, taming the urge to drag her across my thighs and spank her ass. "There's no need to talk to me like that. Did you completely forget the conversation we had a little while ago?"

"What conversation?"

I held her gaze. "The one where I explained that I'm a dominant who likes to be obeyed."

She sighed. "Well I'm not your submissive so I'm not sure that matters much."

"Oh, it matters."

"Says who?"

"Says *me*."

"You're lying." She gave me a smug look.

I'd had it. I knew she was testing, needing to see how I'd react. I reached for her arm and pulled her to me, and pushed her up against the arm of the couch. She flailed her arms, but I was bigger and stronger and she was no match for me. Before I'd even processed what I was doing or how she'd react, I reared back and slapped her ass, hard, once, twice, three times.

"You've got something else to say to me?" I asked.

"You're a brute!" she screamed, but oddly, she didn't get up from where she was but stayed laying over the arm of the couch, despite the fact that I wasn't holding her down anymore. Slowly, so slowly at first I couldn't believe what I was seeing, her legs parted.

So that was how it was going to go?

I leaned in so my mouth was up close to her ear, and I did what I'd been wanting to do since the moment I laid eyes on her—wove my fingers through her long, silky, gorgeous hair, wrapped it around my hand, and pulled, lifting her head just enough that her mouth parted open and her eyes closed with a soft, "ohhh."

"A brute, am I?" I whispered in her ear. "A brute for spanking your ass?"

She panted now as I tugged a bit harder, and hands gripping the edge of the couch so hard her knuckles were white. "Yes," she whispered. "Such… a… brute."

"But something tells me you're the kind of girl who likes a brute, baby. Aren't you?"

Her only response was a low moan that made my cock twitch. I pushed her feet further apart with the tip of my toe, and took in the gorgeous curve of her ass, the full, creamy thighs, and the beautiful, dimpled small of her back. I released her hair and wrapped my hand around her waist, but this time I took my time.

"What did I tell you about obeying?" I said, my low rumble making her bite her lip.

"You said..." her voice was breathless as she rose on her tiptoes, eager for her spanking. "You said... you said I had listen."

Smack. My palm smacked straight across her ass.

"Consider this your warning," I bit out before I landed another swat where her thighs met her ass. "Next time?" A third swat followed. "I'll spank your bare ass."

She let out the most adorable little squeak I ever heard, before she tipped her head to the side and whispered, "Why do I have to wait until next time?" She inhaled but then breathed out in a quick breath, as if she were afraid she'd lose her courage if she didn't speak her mind, "I need it now."

"Excuse me?"

"Ow!" She went up on her tiptoes with a much harder smack than I'd given her yet.

"Please!" she gasped.

"When you talk to me, you say *Sir*. Say that. *Please, Sir.*"

"Oooooh my God," she moaned to herself, before her voice rose. "Please, Sir!"

"Very good," I whispered, hooking the top of her panties with my thumbs and drawing them down over her luscious curves, so slowly she whimpered. The intoxicating musk of her arousal enveloped me, her thighs damp as I gently drew the thin fabric to her ankles.

"Step out of them."

She obeyed quickly, and I rewarded her obedience with a possessive swipe up her inner thigh, pausing at the apex before I drew a finger through her folds. She stilled, even her breathing stopping.

"It's okay, babe," I whispered, gently stroking her. "It's normal to feel aroused when you're dominated. There's nothing wrong with this." I leaned in and kissed her temple gently, not able to stop myself from showing tenderness when the woman was so vulnerable like this. "Let yourself go. Feel it. It'll help you relax. Just do it."

She moaned a low, delicious sound I felt in my groin, and ground herself against my hand as I went faster, her body tensing beneath my touch, her breath coming in choppy gasps as I stroked and circled.

"Let yourself go, now. That's a girl. Take what's yours."

Seconds later she was climaxing, soft little breathy gasps escaping her, her back arching as I stroked her to completion.

"Fuck yeah. That's a good girl. Come for me, baby." She grasped the side of the couch and writhed against my hand, her whole body spasming in ecstasy and when she was done, she collapsed against the arm of the couch. I sat down and drew her onto my lap, holding her up against me. I expected she'd be a bit emotional after that. She was new to this, and I didn't want to push too hard. I'd never planned on going this far with her.

"Wow," she panted. "My God. Ryder, that was amazing."

She pulled even closer to me, burrowing herself in my arms. "Not so sure that should've ended that way. I mean, now you're always going to disobey me," I quipped.

She laughed and lifted her head, looking me in the eyes. "I'm afraid if disobeying you gets me spanked and then you do *that* to me, I *will* have a really hard time doing what I'm told."

I frowned. "I don't think I spanked you hard enough then."

Her eyes went half lidded. "I've barely recovered and you're trying to work me up again?"

"You're incorrigible."

"Not incorrigible! In fact, I think I just haven't been spanked enough."

"Or hard enough. Maybe next time I'll use my belt…"

"Oh my God!"

I grinned. "Do you think you're ready for some sleep now?"

She sighed and leaned against me. "I do feel sleepier. A little confused but sleepy. I'm not sure how I can possibly fall asleep though."

I held her for a little while. I knew this was all new to her, and it didn't surprise me at all she found it a bit confusing. "I know you've been pretty sheltered."

"Understatement of the year."

I snorted. "Yeah. Have you had any alcohol of any sort? Wine? Beer? Mixed drinks? Sometimes that helps you sleep."

She shook her head. "No, but that's all the more reason for me to try it. Bring it!"

I smiled at her. "Say please."

"Please?"

I gently pushed her to the couch. God, I loved this side of her, the adventurous, fearless girl. I got a bottle of wine from the wine cabinet in my kitchen, removed the cork, and poured her a small glass. She'd have to start slowly, as I didn't want her getting sick on it. But it would help her sleep, maybe.

I poured a larger glass for myself, and went in to see her.

She was nestled up in the corner of the couch, looking to me expectantly. "Here. Try this. Sip it *slowly.*"

She nodded, and took the glass, eyeing the pale, yellow liquid with a curious eye. She sniffed it and took a tentative sip. "That's delicious," she said, then took another sip and another.

"What'd I say about sipping slowly?"

She frowned. "I swallowed it slowly." Her eyes met mine in challenge. I placed my glass down and leaned over, taking her glass out of her hand and placing it on the table, then grasped her chin and looked in her eyes. "Did you?" I asked.

"The issue is that you really like to push boundaries, babe," I said, releasing her chin and wrapping my hand around the back of her neck, pulling her close to me. "You need to learn to obey the rules."

She swallowed, her breath shallow, her pupils dilated. My cock strained for release, needing to claim this woman.

Her breath was so close to me now I could feel the warmth grazing my skin as she whispered up at me, "Do the rules allow for kissing?"

I responded by taking her mouth with mine, pulling her close, my hand tightening on her neck. She'd never experienced any of this before, and she hesitated at first, not knowing what to do, but I showed her by taking her. I would claim this woman, make her mine. I hadn't had a submissive in so long, I'd almost forgotten what it felt like to have the push and pull. I'd taken all kinds of submissives, but I loved when a woman was strong enough to stand up to me, to really challenge me.

I pulled my mouth off hers, though it killed me to do so. I wanted to sink into her, lose myself. "God, you're beautiful, you know that?"

She shook her head. "I have no reference point, really."

I laughed out loud. "Baby, you're beautiful." She sat on my

lap, her t-shirt barely covering her bare ass, the white panties still pooled on the floor. "How's that wine treating you?"

She tipped her head to the side. "It's so weird. My head feels lighter and it seems like my words are louder and muffled all at the same time. Funny, huh? I don't get it at all."

"Sounds about right," I said. "Warm? Do you feel warm anywhere?" I asked, laying her down on the couch so her back was flat against it and I pressed my body over hers.

"Only every inch of me."

I grinned. "Is that the alcohol, or something else?"

She chuckled, a low, seductive laugh that hit me straight in the groin. "I have no idea. Not a clue. But whatever it is, please don't stop. It's making me forget everything. Help me forget please, Ryder."

Part of me knew I shouldn't be doing this. The girl was an innocent virgin ignorant to the ways of the world. She'd never been kissed or touched or even walked outside her house alone and here I was straddling her on my couch, plying her with wine after I'd spanked her ass and made her come. But when she asked me like that, when she begged me to help her forget what troubled her, I couldn't help but give her what she asked me for.

I sobered at her request and brought my mouth to her ear. "I have toys in the bedroom, Rae. Lots of things that can help make you forget. The club is closed downstairs, and I could bring you down and show you all sorts of things that will take you to another level. And it's my pleasure to do that."

She looked at me, more serious now. "Really?" she whispered.

"Really, babe," I whispered back.

She closed her eyes, as if she couldn't hold them open anymore, and hugged me closer. "But this is nice. I don't want to leave here. I don't even want to go to that big, huge bed alone. It's warm here. And safe."

"We don't need to do any of those things tonight. Tonight, you'll have a little more wine, and then I'll bring you to bed. You need rest, and tomorrow's another day."

She nodded. "Yes. Thank you, Ryder."

I kissed her temple and sat her up, brushing the hair off her forehead and tucking a stray lock behind her ear. "Have one more glass of wine," I said. "It'll help you relax a bit." I tipped more of the cool liquid into her glass and handed it to her, marveling at how she sat there without a care, one curvy leg tucked under her ass. She didn't try to cover herself up like other girls did. It surprised me at first, but as I watched her, I realized that somehow, having not experienced the outside world, she hadn't learned to be inhibited. I swallowed hard as she sipped the liquid, watching her nipples peek through the thin fabric of my t-shirt.

I'd never look at the t-shirt the same again.

"What kinds of books do you like to read, Ryder?" she asked, her head tipped to the side as she watched me.

The question surprised me. "Excuse me?"

"You have books in your room and a huge collection out here."

I smiled. "I read anything and everything. I like mysteries and suspense and fantasy, non-fiction, memoirs. Things like that."

"Romance?"

I laughed out loud. "Um, no."

She smiled. "Guess you don't read *every* kind of book then."

"Guess not." I watched as she emptied her glass again.

"Christ, Rae. I told you not to drink so fast."

She shrugged. "Why not?"

"First, because I told you not to."

JANE HENRY

Her eyes came to mine and she sobered, her voice dropping. "Would you spank me again?"

I swallowed, my hand itching to tame her naughty ass. "Fuck yeah I would. But you have to understand you could get sick drinking too much too fast." I took her glass out of her hand and placed it on the coffee table then fixed her with a stern look that made her squirm.

"No more."

She crossed her arms on her chest and stared at me, as if trying to figure out how to respond. We were beginning, still feeling each other out, but she'd learn I meant what I said. I tipped a finger under her chin and got her attention. "I didn't hear your response."

Her eyes widened a bit but challenged me, still, not softening but probing. "What am I supposed to say again?"

"Some say Master. Some say Daddy. For now, we'll stick with Sir."

She looked at me from beneath lowered lashes. "Yes, Sir," she whispered. My chest swelled with the sound of it. Even though I'd directed her to call me *Sir,* hearing her still made me want to take her, hard, to show her that fuck yeah, I was someone who would master her.

She leaned back against the couch and closed her eyes. "I feel tired now, Ryder. I think that... wine... really hit me." Her words were slurred. Yeah, the wine hit her alright.

"Alright. Off to bed with you. Let's go." I stood and reached for her, pulling her to her feet and half carrying her as she leaned her full weight on me. Fortunately, it was only a few steps to the bedroom. I took her in and turned down the comforter, and she knelt up on the bed and slid under the sheets. I tucked the blanket around her, as if it somehow symbolized a layer of protection I would give her, a defense against the dangers that surrounded her.

"Will you stay just a minute?" she whispered, her eyes already closing.

"Of course." I ran my hand down the length of her soft, sweet hair, then raked my fingers through once more. She sighed in contentment, and snuggled deeper under the covers. I stayed there like that for a few minutes, gently rubbing her back and stroking her hair until her breathing slowed and I watched the rise and fall of the blankets as she slept.

"I'll be right outside your door if you need me," I whispered, though I knew she couldn't hear me. It felt nice to say it though. She'd be safe with me. I had no idea what I would do with her or where we'd go from here, or even if she'd remember this in the morning, but for now, I would give her whatever I could.

RAE

When I woke the next morning, the light streaming through the window indicated that daylight had long since broken. It felt a little weird, since I never slept this late. As I sat up in bed, I rubbed my eyes, wondering what time it was. Not that it mattered. I wasn't home anymore. I wouldn't have to wait for the sounds of my father going to work, or taking a conference call before I went down to breakfast to avoid seeing or talking to him.

As I shifted in the bed, my ass stung, and I suddenly remembered with vivid clarity. I closed my eyes, a pulse of arousal licking through me like flames to paper, starting slowly, then spreading rapidly. My head felt a bit fuzzy, but my body... my body remembered. My ass was warm, and stung, but for some reason I liked that it did. I was never spanked, even as a child, and it puzzled me that I liked that Ryder spanked me. But then again, he had an entire club of people who came here for a bit of release. Maybe Ryder would be willing to talk to me about it...

The memory of his eyes clouding over, as he pulled me by the wrist and spread me over the side of the couch, had me squirming. Before I could indulge in much more than that brief memory, a knock came at the door frame.

I pulled the covers up to my chin, which was silly considering he'd seen me practically naked the night before. Ryder entered, looking all kinds of sexy wearing nothing but the same pair of boxers he wore last night. My tummy fluttered just looking at him as he walked toward me, his dark hair tousled and his blue, blue eyes piercing. He had a shadow of stubble on his jaw, which he scrubbed a hand across while he looked at me, and my eyes traveled the length of him, down his muscled shoulders, honed abs, and the little trail of dark hair that dipped lower still. I swallowed hard.

"Morning," he said, his voice all sleep-sexy.

"Morning," I responded, my own voice strangely husky.

"You sleep okay?" he asked. I nodded. I'd slept well after he finally helped me relax, and now I felt my stomach rumble in hunger.

"I'm good, just hungry."

He nodded and ran a hand through his hair, which only mussed it up more, then he crossed his arms. "How are you feeling about last night?" He leaned against the doorframe and frowned.

"About last night?" I looked away, though I didn't want to stop looking at him. There was something intimate and sexy about his early morning tousled look. I cleared my throat. "A lot happened last night. For starters, I'm glad I'm no longer home, if that's what you mean."

I looked back at him. He grunted, his voice a low rumble. "Figured that much."

"Oh. Well, then everything else was... fine." My ass burned, my stomach dipped, and I pulled the blanket tighter under my chin.

He raised a curious brow, then nodded. "Your head okay?"

I cleared my throat. "It hurts a little."

"You'll have some water in a few minutes to help that." His lips quirked a bit then. "Your ass?"

I couldn't help but smile shyly. "My ass is fine, thank you for asking."

He pushed himself off the doorframe and walked into the living room, talking over his shoulder. "Too bad. I was hoping it still stung a little so you'd remember to behave yourself today."

I laughed to myself, tossing off the blanket, and he yelled out to me again. "Come on out here. I've got some clothes for you to choose from."

Feeling a bit shy but excited, I left the room and followed him out to his living room. A huge, light pink bag sat on the overstuffed chair, and several others beside it. "Had an associate pick out some clothes for you. Grab something you're comfortable in. We'll eat breakfast, then you're going to meet with a member of my staff. She's a hairstylist."

My stomach plummeted to my feet, but I hid my surprise and discomfort by taking the boxes out of the bags, and opening them. I wore simple, classic clothing at home, t-shirts and jeans mostly, and here were some similar outfits. I pulled out several pairs of yoga pants and dark-colored jeans, a few pretty sweaters. Simple clothes, but ones that I liked. They were comfortable and well made, and wouldn't make me stand out in a crowd.

I needed that.

I pulled out a pair of jeans and a light green long-sleeved top, then saw a smaller bag at the bottom of the pile. In there I found two packages of panties, several bras, and socks. I took out what I needed, feeling a bit embarrassed knowing Ryder had given instructions for someone to purchase these, and turned to face him. He held a cup of coffee up to his lips, watching me. I swallowed. There was something in his eyes I couldn't decipher, but I suspected I wasn't the only one who remembered what had happened the night before with such clarity.

"Need to find out who the man was who took you is."

I nodded, both sadness and relief coming to me at once. I hated that things were going to change, but I knew that they needed to. The only person I'd ever known, the man who raised me, was likely a criminal, this much I'd gathered. Though I'd been kept apart from the world, I wasn't completely ignorant. I knew that he was in regular contact with the police force. I knew that he spoke in hushed tones with men in his office, and that he employed several large, scary-looking men who weren't allowed to talk or come near me. And I knew the way he'd treated me was anything but healthy.

"Yes. Of course." I turned away from Ryder, hiding the unshed tears that flooded my eyes. "May I go take a shower now?"

"Yeah. You'll find everything you need in there. Make it quick. I want to eat breakfast, and then we meet Francesca in an hour."

Francesca?

"I can't wash my hair and be ready to go in an hour. Do you have any idea how long it takes me to wash this?" I held it up to him to remind him. "*Some* of us have more than a one-inch spikes all over our heads."

He placed his coffee cup down on the table slowly, his gaze not meeting mine, as I continued. "So you can't rush me like that."

"Don't wash your hair," he said, now stalking over to me. I didn't realize I was backing up until my back hit a chair.

"I can't *not wash my hair*. Are you crazy? After all I've been through? I have to."

My fists curled at my sides, and I was angry at him. Why was I acting like such a child?

When he reached me, I let out a little yelp as he wove his hand through my hair and tugged, just enough that my body flamed at his touch, my mouth falling open with a little gasp.

"Watch your tone, Rae."

I closed my eyes, melting into his touch as he took over once again.

"What tone?" I snapped. "There is no tone."

He tugged my hair harder, his voice firm. "What'd I say about lying?"

I let out a shuddering breath. "You said not to. You said there would be trust between us."

"Then don't lie to me."

I inhaled, then exhaled slowly. This was what I wanted. This was what I *needed.* Then why did I fight it so hard?

"Fine. You're right. My tone was rude. I'm hungry, and scared, and I'm alone with a man who makes my body come to life at the mere sound of his voice. Is that honest enough for you?"

He pulled me closer. "Baby."

"And I don't know what will happen from one minute to the next. I have no control over my reactions, no control over my future... no control over *anything.*"

"Rae."

I opened my eyes and looked up at him, his gaze both stern and gentle. How did he do that?

He let my hair go and cupped my jaw with his strong hand, bending his head. My heart fluttered, my breath coming in rapid gasps, seconds before his mouth met mine. This time, his kiss was gentle, soothing, nothing like the rough claiming of the night before, but still my body rose to meet him, my breasts swelling, wanting more. When he pulled his mouth off mine I whimpered a little. "You are strong," he said, tapping my chin. "You are brave. After today, you will have a better idea where we will go from here. But listen to me." His voice sobered. "Did you hear me?"

He tucked me up against his chest in a hug, his strength awakening my need. I breathed in deep and squared my shoulders when he let me go. "Now go take your shower."

I walked to the shower, grabbed a fluffy towel from one of the shelves, and noticed that he'd stocked the shower with a variety of girly toiletries I hadn't seen the day before. They looked like nice enough toiletries, so I grabbed a washcloth and some soap and quickly showered, then came out leaving my hair dry and unwashed. Washing my hair was an all-day affair, and I didn't have the luxury of time today. And then I realized with a twinge of sadness this was likely the last day I'd have my trademark hair.

But it was time to move on, to start my new life.

I dressed quickly, and came out to the dining room where Ryder passed me.

"I'm gonna get dressed. Grab something to eat. I didn't know what you liked so I put out a little bit of everything."

This was new. At home, I was on a strictly regulated diet. I was never allowed to eat sweets, or processed food. So when I spied a tray of pastries, I knew exactly what I was going to eat. I chose a figure-eight shaped pastry filled with cream cheese and some sort of preserves, and a bowl of sliced berries. The smell of coffee wafted in from the kitchen. I wondered what that tasted like...

Was I some kind of child, who'd never been allowed to sample what others did? It made me angry, so when Ryder came out and asked if I'd found what I liked, I snapped.

"Yes, obviously. But I'd like a cup of coffee."

I couldn't keep the anger out of my voice, though it wasn't directed at him. So much of what I felt had been bottled up for so long I wasn't sure how to deal with it.

He frowned. "If you found something to eat, then why do you look so pissed off?"

I chewed the pastry angrily. "I don't really know. I'm not angry at you. In fact, I'm kind of embarrassed about how I'm behaving right now, because you've been nothing but good to me, and I don't even really know why you have. I just feel..."

I clenched my fists, fighting the angry tears that threatened to spill. "It all started because I smelled coffee, and I've never been allowed to taste it in my *fucking* life. And yes, I just swore. I'm not allowed to swear either. And it's ridiculous. I'm twenty years old, and I've been treated like a ten-year-old my entire life, and I know I don't want that anymore."

A knock came at the door. "Just a minute!" Ryder shouted. Then he leaned down to me and to my surprise, he kissed my cheek, then whispered in my ear, "Rae, there's a lot that you're going to have to work on probably for a very long time. Today is going to be hard for you. You're going to lose a part of yourself, a part of your identity, and you're going to discuss some very uncomfortable things. But there's something you need to understand. Last night showed me that I want to get to know you better. That you will trust me, and that I might be able to help give you what you need." He threaded his hand through my hair and tugged. I closed my eyes, sighing, it felt so nice, though it stung a little. "I know that you respond well to this," he whispered. "So today, I want you to do your best. Be as strong as you can. And tonight, I'm going to reward you."

He let me go and walked to the door. I smoothed my hands along my thighs, willing myself to calm down. One night with Ryder, and I already knew that any reward would be well worth it.

When he opened the door, I didn't know what to expect, but it definitely wasn't a tall, beautiful woman with a mane of vibrant red curls, bright green eyes, and a smattering of freckles across her cheeks. She came in pushing a cart.

"Hello, Master Ryder."

Ryder reaction was a bit surprising. He frowned. The stern but kind man I'd spent the night with had become cold, aloof. "What did I tell you about calling me Master outside of the dungeon?"

"But we're still in the club." She walked past him, and extended her hand to me. "Hello. You must be Rae. I'm Francesca."

"For Christ's sake," Ryder muttered. "Who told you her name? You're not to call her by name."

She blinked and stammered, "I—I'm sorry Mas—Sir. Dean mentioned you had a girl named Rae who needed some help with her hair."

Ryder raked his hand through his dark hair, making some of it stand up at odd angles. He didn't look silly, though. He looked sexy and sorta roguish. He shoved his hands in his pockets. A muscle ticked in his jaw. "I'm sorry. It's not your fault, then. I just need to keep Rae under wraps. She'll go by a different name here."

I looked at him in surprise. We hadn't discussed this yet, but I thought having an alternative name would be a really good idea.

"I'll be..." I said, immediately thinking of my favorite storybook character Anne Shirley because I was standing in the presence of a drop-dead gorgeous redhead. "Anne."

His eyes twinkled and one lip quirked up. "Anne with an e?"

"Yes, please." I smiled shyly at him as Francesca busied herself with lining up a plastic cape, combs, scissors, and a spray bottles.

"As you can see, she has beautiful hair but unfortunately

it's a very identifying characteristic. We're going to have to cut it off." I ignored the little flip my tummy did.

Francesca's face fell. "I'm so sorry to hear that. It really is stunningly beautiful. What can I do for you?"

I swallowed hard but didn't blink when I looked at her. "I want you to cut it all off. I want it short… to my chin." My voice wavered a bit.

Ryder peered at me, and crossed his arms on his chest. "You sure about that?"

I nodded. "Yes. Please."

"Okay, Rae… I mean, Anne," Francesca said, coming around to stand in front of me. "We'll move to the bathroom for easy clean up, and get things started. You ready?"

I inhaled and squared my shoulders, then nodded. "Yes," I said softly. "I'm ready."

Ryder's large, warm hand slid into mine, and he squeezed. A look flitted across Francesca's face, but she didn't say anything, just gathered up her things and made her way to the bathroom.

I noted that she knew where his room was. Yeah, he only had a small place, but still. She'd been here before. There was a familiarity to her walk.

She'd been his submissive at one point. I felt it. A sick sort of feeling wove its way through my gut as I followed them.

"Any idea what kind of haircut you want, Rae— I mean, Anne?" Her cheeks flushed and she looked quickly at Ryder. His jaw clenched but he said nothing.

"I have no idea. Something radically different would be good."

"A bob?"

"Christ, a *bob?*" Ryder said. "God, no. Do something choppy and layered. Something sexy that accentuates her gorgeous cheek bones." He released my hand and pointed to the toilet for me to sit.

"You sure you want that?" Francesca asked, and I nodded.

"Yeah, I just want this done." I didn't look at either of them. They were weird together. I might not have been wise to the ways of the world, but I knew that they'd had something, and it was uncomfortable.

"And black," I said. "Let's go for black, shoulder length, layered, long bangs in front. I like the sound of that."

Francesca grinned. "I do, too. I have some color-tinting contacts, and we'll do your makeup quite dramatically. Tonight, you'll be introduced as Master Ryder's submissive." Her voice caught a bit at that, confirming my suspicions.

"Perfect," Ryder said. "I'm going downstairs to check on things. Got a meeting with Seth and Dean. You call me if you need me." He frowned and looked at me. "I'll have two men at the door. I mean it when I say call if you need me. Got it?"

I swallowed and nodded.

When the door clicked behind him a moment later, Francesca leaned in and her eyes met mine.

"I'm sorry about that. It was awkward. It *is* awkward."

"What's awkward?" I asked, while she stood and began spraying my hair with water, drawing a thick comb through the length. "This is a detangler," she said, clearly evading my question. "God, this hair is beautiful. Have you considered donating it?"

"Wait a minute. You didn't tell me what was awkward yet."

She sighed and sprayed my hair, drawing her long comb through it. "Me. Him. *Us*. That's what's awkward."

A little pang of jealousy pricked me. "Oh? Were you... dating?"

I couldn't see her face, because she now stood behind me, but her tone was both reminiscent and sad. "Master Ryder and I didn't work out," she said.

I didn't ask any questions. I didn't want to know. We sat

there in silence, until finally she broke the silence. "I asked if you wanted to donate your hair?"

"Oh, right. Donating it? People do that?"

"Oh yes. When people get sick and lose their hair, with chemo or something, they sometimes need a wig, but those are pricey. Sometimes people who cut off their long hair are able to donate it to places that will treat it and make a wig for those who need it. I worked at one place for years."

So my tragedy could become someone else's luck.

"Well, yeah, let's do that," I said.

She left the bathroom and came back a few minutes later with a large sheet. "Ryder doesn't need to know we used this. He might not be too happy about his perfect sheets on the bathroom floor." She winked, her tone derisive, and she tossed the sheet down.

Maybe I could see why she didn't get along so well with Ryder.

"Okay, honey. You ready?"

I nodded, and sudden tears pricked my eyes at the sight of the sharp shears in her hand, swinging my gaze to focus on the large whirlpool tub. I blinked hard.

"Damn, I wish he'd stayed. You look like you're about to cry."

"Yeah," I whispered, not trusting my voice.

She sighed. "Okay. Keep your hands folded in your lap. Here we go." At that, I felt the first snip of the scissors, and a great weight fell away. I sat in silence, as she stripped away a part of who I was. I closed my eyes, willing myself to be brave. It had to be done.

RYDER

I HATED LEAVING Rae and Francesca alone. Francesca wouldn't hurt Rae. I trusted her that much at least. But we'd had a relationship, and it fell flat. I wondered if Rae would ask questions, and how Francesca would respond. Francesca was loyal, though. And trustworthy. But I knew Rae was in a very vulnerable place.

"Any read on her father?" I asked Dean. I leaned against the edge of my desk in my office, looking at both Seth and Dean who'd been waiting for me when I arrived. "Caden find anything?" I'd looked him up myself, and knew his name was Martel, but his track record was clean.

Seth shook his head, his dark eyes stormy. Caden had connections with the local police department, and I knew he could tread lightly, since we didn't want anyone probing into our business.

"Says there's no record of the guy having any affiliation with the police department, but that he knows a few other people he can ask, people who are more likely to know more of what's off the record."

I nodded. "Keep me posted."

JANE HENRY

"Always, boss." Seth's dark eyes probed mine. "How is she?"

"She's good," I said, not able to make eye contact with him. He couldn't know I'd taken advantage of her the way I did. It was best if no one knew a damn thing about her, but it was too hard to keep *everything* quiet.

"You all set?" I asked Dean, who nodded his head.

"Yeah. Got a new name and address and I.D. You said Anne, so we went with that. My man's finalizing paperwork now, and we'll get that all underway. He also has a team of people who work for him intentionally spreading rumors about the new Anne who's come to Limits."

"Rumors?" I didn't like the sound of that one bit.

"Nothing bad," he said. "Just that she's your new submissive, and keeps to herself."

I didn't like any attention drawn to her at all, even though I asked for this, but I knew how people were. If they didn't get any information, they'd make things up, and it was better to steer them away from the truth. I hated playing games like this, but it seemed the best way to protect her.

"Fair enough. Let me know as soon as you find anything else about her father."

Seth didn't answer at first, which caught my attention. He was always the most attentive, alert member of my staff, and if he was focused on something else, then it was likely worthwhile to note.

"Something on your mind, Seth?" I asked.

He stroked his chin, and turned back to me. "Something very familiar about the guy's name," he said. "It isn't his real name, we've figured that much out. Not surprising, either, considering that he had a girl he kidnapped under his roof. How old did you say she was again?"

"Twenty or so," I said. She should've been in college, second year, ready to make her way in the world instead of holed up in some sick bastard's tower. "He's likely fabricated her age, too, so he can keep her under wraps. Who knows what the guy's lied about."

"Right," Seth said. "For now, I'm gonna ask around. See if anyone knows anything. I have a few people who might be able to shed some light."

"Perfect."

I opened up the calendar on the desktop and looked at our assigned stations. "Tonight, I'm supposed to be taking my shift supervising the dungeon, but I want to be sure I'm available for Rae—I mean Anne. She's undergoing a major change, and I'm not sure how she's going to handle things. She was kind of a mess last night." *Until I spanked the sass right out of her and made her climax.*

Plus, tonight I'd promised her a reward if she behaved herself. I had plans.

I cleared my throat and both Dean and Seth nodded, Dean pushing himself to his feet.

"Happy to take over the dungeon shift tonight, boss," he said. "You game for that?"

Dean had only trained with us for six months, and most who took the dungeon shift, where the heavier play took place, were trained for far longer. But he could be trusted, so I nodded.

"Yeah, consider it your training," I said. "Week one." I turned to Seth. "Be sure you go over protocol with him and report back to me every half hour. Understood?"

"Yes, sir," both men said in unison. I got to my feet and checked my phone. A text message waited for me.

All done. She looks lovely, but is a bit unnerved by the whole thing. Come see?

I cleared my throat and put my phone in my pocket. "I'll check in this evening. Let me know the second you hear anything else."

I took my leave, nervous anticipation weaving its way through me. What would she look like? I'd already grown to love her long, beautiful hair, the way it swung about her like a sort of crown or veil. I'd never seen anything like it. I decided as I made my way up to see her that no matter what, I'd like her new look. Everything about her was beautiful. How could a haircut really make that much of a difference?

When the doors of the elevator opened, I walked the length of the hall, and a flash outside the hall window caught my attention. I peered down below and cupped a hand over my eyes, squinting. I watched as Dean's SUV peeled off out of the parking lot. That was weird. I knew after our meeting he had an eight-hour stint ahead of him. Why would he leave so suddenly?

I texted Seth. *Where's Dean going?*

Shoving my phone in my pocket, I punched in the code to let me in the apartment and the door unlocked with an audible click. I turned the knob and opened the door. With years of experience cultivating the role of a Dominant, I'd learned to school my features.

"Hello? Girls?" I called out. I walked from the living area to the bedroom. The door to the bathroom was wide open, and it didn't take long to see they were gone.

Panic rose in my chest, and I clenched my fists. Had someone hurt them? There were no signs of a struggle, so I reasoned they must have left. I wanted to spank both their asses until they couldn't sit for a fucking week.

I'd told them to stay. Francesca had *called me* back and summoned me to come see. Where had they gone?

"Hello?" As time passed, I began to worry that something had happened. I grabbed my phone and texted Francesca. *Where the hell are you?*

But there was no reply. After going through every room in my apartment one more time, I'd just decided I'd go back down to Limits and check the security cameras, when a soft knock came at the door.

I peeked through the peephole, my hands shaking, and almost didn't recognize the girl with black hair who stood there, but she blinked back up at me with the same brown eyes I'd come to adore. I yanked open the door, and before she said a word, took her by the hand and pulled her in the apartment.

"Get in here," I said, my voice betraying my anger. "What the fuck do you think you're doing?

"Why are you mad?" Her eyes flashed at me.

"You're damn right I'm mad." I slammed the door behind her. "Where's Francesca?"

"Downstairs."

"Why didn't you stay here?" I asked. For Christ's sake, didn't anyone do anything they were supposed to?

Her eyes flashed at me. "I did," she said. "I got my hair cut and dyed. I went downstairs with Francesca to get some more supplies, and you walked right past me. What the hell is your problem, Ryder?"

I pulled her to me, needing to teach her a lesson for the way she talked to me, for mouthing off like that. I pulled her toward me. "Is that any way to talk to me? And who told you to leave this place?" I asked, running my hands up her neck and threading my fingers through the short black locks. I held onto my control by a mere thread. She looked nothing like herself, but the shiny hair smelled deliciously fragrant and clean, and the dark color illuminated her wide eyes and full lips. "God, you look fucking beautiful," I said, drawing her closer and taking her mouth with mine. Like a match set to tinder, she lit up, melting into me, every inch of her body flush against mine, asking for more, needing me to take her. Our lips met briefly before I pulled away, leaned up against the side of the couch, spun her out, and yanked her across my knee.

"Ryder! My God!"

I ignored her protest, took the little hand that flailed back to protect her ass, and pinned it to her lower back. "You don't mouth off to me," I said, slapping her ass hard, "And for God's sake, I told you not to leave this apartment. You think I'm fooling around? You think this is some kind of a joke?"

"No! God, no." She writhed over my lap, but I didn't let her go until I'd administered a dozen hard smacks. Even with jeans on, she'd feel that for a while.

"Not giving you another chance, Rae. You think you can handle this shit? Well I'm not taking that risk. You'll do what I fucking say."

I stood her up and planted her in front of me. Grasping her forearms, I gave her a little shake. She nodded, her lips parted in surprise. "I get it," she said. "I get it!"

"Good. I'll deal with Francesca later." I let her go. "Where the fuck did you go?"

"Downstairs in the conference room she had a few more supplies. Some makeup and stuff. Not that you noticed." Her chin jutted out.

"Rae, go sit down. I've got shit to figure out."

But she didn't move. She crossed her arms on her chest and glared at me.

Seriously? Maybe I *didn't* spank hard enough.

"Excuse me? What did I just tell you to do?"

"What do you *mean* you'll take care of Francesca later?" She glared.

I blinked. What the fuck?

"Rae, she's my employee. She put you at risk with her stupidity, and yeah, she'll deal with me. My staff is expected to do what I fucking tell them to do. You have a problem with that?"

"So you'll spank her, too?" She crossed her arms over her chest and continued to glare.

"What? No! Do you think I just go around spanking my staff whenever I want?" Christ. I planted my hands on my hips and glared.

She looked a little embarrassed then. "Well. No, not exactly…"

"I'm their boss. I expect them to listen to me. If they don't, they answer to me. That's all. I expect my employees to do what I say. I don't spank them. I spanked *you*. And you better fucking watch your tone of voice, unless you want a repeat."

She stood and glared at me, not moving.

"Francesca said you were a couple," she said, "Did you spank her, Ryder? Huh? Did you? Did you make her climax, too?" Her eyes gleamed with unshed tears. "Did you tell *her* she was beautiful and special?"

Jesus. The girl was *jealous*. I didn't know if I should laugh, spank her *bare* ass, or fuck her up against the wall and show her exactly what I thought about her.

She was jealous of *Francesca*, a girl I'd taken to a cousin's wedding once three years earlier. We'd never been a thing.

I crossed my arms over my chest. "You know what, little girl?"

"Why did you call me *that*?" she asked, throwing her hands up in the air. "Like… like… you're my *Daddy* or something."

Just hearing her say *my Daddy* made my cock hard. I swallowed hard and adjusted myself, my voice husky and deep when I spoke. "Like I'm your Daddy. Yeah, babe. I like that." I crooked a finger at her. "C'mere."

Her eyes cast down at the floor and her full, beautiful lower lip stuck out. I needed to take that lip between my teeth and taste it. But I'd wait.

She dragged her feet as she came to me, likely aware that

she deserved to be spanked for her behavior, and that I wouldn't hesitate to punish her. But she needed more than punishment. We were new, and I'd fucked up.

I sat down on the couch, and pulled her onto my lap. She stiffened, but I rubbed a hand on her back, slowly circling the soft fabric of her sweater. I felt the bump of her bra underneath, and my cock pushed up against her ass. I inhaled deeply. I needed to get a grip on things before I fucked this up even more.

"Rae. I'm sorry."

Her eyes met mine with curiosity, "You are?" she asked softly.

"Yeah, honey. I've jumped into this and broken the cardinal rule."

"What's that?" she whispered.

"Communication."

She didn't say anything at first, just nodded.

"A few things first. I never dated Francesca. She isn't my type. It never would've worked, and I never would've pursued it, and honestly, honey, if she was an ex of mine, I wouldn't have left her up here alone with you."

She relaxed a bit up against my chest. "Isn't your type?" she asked in a whisper. "Is she too… strong? You like more submissive women?"

I chuckled, running my hands through her beautiful, jet black hair. "No, babe. She's too *submissive*. Some guys, they dig girls like her. I could name a dozen. But I like someone who'll give me a challenge. I want someone who'll make me *earn* their submission. I don't want it handed to me like it's free for the taking."

"Oh." Her voice was so low I could hardly hear her. "So you… like… that I'm not completely submissive."

"Hell yeah," I growled. "There's fire in your eyes. You're a girl who knows what she wants, and won't back down for anything. I'd have thought someone who was treated the way you were would lose part of her self-worth, her confidence. But no. It's made you stronger. Braver. Feistier."

She grinned and bit her lip. "Well... if I behave too well, I won't get spanked, and I..." her voice trailed off as she ran a finger down my chest and played with the button on my shirt. "I like when you spank me."

I huffed out a laugh. "Even when I punish you? Like I just did now?"

She closed her eyes and her words came out in a breathy whisper. "*Especially* then."

I squeezed her close. Tonight, I'd show her a whole new world, a side of things she'd maybe read about but had never experienced.

"So we're back to square one," I quipped, landing a sharp slap to her bottom.

She laughed. "Oh?"

"How am I supposed to teach you to behave if you like when I punish you?"

She giggled. "I think we'll just have to keep trying."

I leaned in and kissed her, my lips just brushing hers before I pulled away. "You'll talk to me, Rae. I have no idea where this is going or what we're doing, but I know the most important thing you can do is talk to me. Tell me what's on your mind. Tell me how you're feeling. Don't bottle it up, or I can't help."

Bearing the burden of another's hopes, fears, and struggles was a difficult but necessary component of being a good Dominant, attentive to the needs of his submissive. I would listen to her. I'd help her. I would teach her.

She would teach me.

Here was a girl who came to me untainted by the ways of the world, eager to submit to me, eager to learn. She'd have hurdles, past pain to deal with, but we'd deal with the struggles one at a time.

"You said to talk to each other," she said, entwining her fingers in mine and squirming a bit. It wasn't lost on me that she didn't meet my eyes.

"Yeah?"

She cleared her throat and said something so soft I couldn't hear.

"What's that?"

"Well… there's something I need to talk about. I don't understand why I liked it when you said you were like my… *Daddy*."

Hearing her call me *Daddy* made my mouth go dry, my cock twitching against her ass, still hot from the brief spanking I gave her.

"Lots of reasons," I said, squeezing her hand. "I've been doing this a while, and I know that it's hot for some girls. Makes them feel safe. A little taboo, maybe, to call a guy you're attracted to a name that's usually reserved for their father." I squeezed her shoulder. "Something about being with a guy you can trust makes you feel secure, and women are emotional creatures. Some women find it sort of healing to call their Dom Daddy. Some just find it erotic. Many find it both."

She frowned. "But my whole childhood was a mess. I mean, my father isn't even my father, and he was this… control freak."

I kissed her forehead. "Lots of girls call their guy Daddy, babe. It doesn't mean you're fucked up. Listen… we're *all* fucked up somewhere along the line. Here, when you're with me, and you trust me, we can explore ways to help you heal."

"You know, that's a lot of *fucked up's* without actually… fucking. And you know what, Ryder?" She moved on my lap so that her knees faced the couch, and her chest brushed up against mine when she looked up to me. "You know what," she repeated, biting her lip, "Daddy?"

I groaned as she leaned in to me, her full breasts brushing my chest, her eyes half-lidded.

"What, baby girl?" I whispered, weaving my hands through her hair and tugging hard, so that her lips parted open before she licked them.

"I lived my whole life holed up, treated like a little girl. Here, with you, I want to break free from that, erase my past from my memory. Show me, Ryder. Show me what a woman should feel. I want you to give that to me." When I didn't answer at first, she tried once more. "Please? Daddy?"

God, I wanted to, but I'd been experienced enough in the lifestyle and as a Dominant to know that it was my job to make sure she didn't move too fast, especially when what she was experiencing was sort of like a rebound. Emotionally vulnerable, I could easily take advantage of her. I didn't want a quick fuck. Though I wanted her so badly I could fucking taste it, my cock straining for release against her full, beautiful backside, I needed to take my time. Things were moving quickly, and we weren't even close to being out of the woods with her past, still unsure as to how that could affect things.

I'd do my damnedest to make sure it didn't. But I had to be careful.

"I'm going to ask you to trust me, Rae," I said, putting a finger under her chin so that her eyes met mine. "You're special to me. And I want to cherish what we have here. But we can't rush it. Not two days ago, you were kept apart from the world, and this is your first taste of freedom. I need to ease you into this. I don't want you making choices you'll regret. It would be irresponsible of me."

She frowned. "Isn't that up to me?"

I loved how her eyes lit up like that, the fire within her so fucking sexy. She had a point.

I held her chin in my hand and stared into her eyes. "*Always.* We do nothing without your consent. But I want to make sure that consent is informed. Got it?"

She didn't answer at first, but just looked at me, frowning a bit, but her gaze didn't leave mine. Finally, after what seemed like an eternity, she nodded. "Yes," she said, no longer whispering but speaking with conviction. "I trust you." She swallowed. "I trust you, Daddy."

My stomach dipped, pride warming me through. I leaned in at the same time she did, our lips meeting hesitantly at first, then intensifying, only to be interrupted when my phone rang.

Seth's ringtone. I pulled away with reluctance and held a finger up to her.

"Gotta take this, babe."

She nodded, slowly sliding off my lap and watching curiously as I answered my phone. I stifled a groan.

"Ryder. What's up?"

"Got a situation, boss. Found out more about our suspect. Want me to come to you, or do you want to come here?"

I hated the idea of leaving her again.

"Can what you have to tell me be said in front of R–Anne?"

"Absolutely. In fact, we'll need her cooperation to proceed."

"You hear from Dean?"

"Not yet."

I inhaled, then blew out a breath. "Come on up."

"I'll be there in five."

I ended the call and slid the phone onto the table. "That was Seth, one of the men who helped rescue you last night. He needs to fill me in on what they've found, and I suspect it has to do with the guy you lived with." I wouldn't call him her father. "Can you answer some questions for us?"

She raised her chin and nodded. "I'll do the best I can. I promise."

I took her hand in mine, and squeezed. "That's my brave girl."

She grinned at me, her fetching eyes twinkling. "And besides, I have an *excellent* memory. And you promised me that if I behaved, you'd reward me tonight. Still planning on doing that?"

She had *no fucking idea*. "Hell yeah." I had a whole room under lock and key that would be ours, sound-proof and fully equipped. I had some ideas in mind for her.

"Then watch me model perfect behavior. Well..." her voice trailed off.

I rose a brow.

"If I'm perfect, will you spank me?" she whispered.

I nodded. "Misbehave, and Daddy will punish you. Behave, and you'll get the best spanking of your life. Deal?"

She grinned. "That's so confusing. But yes. Yes, Daddy."

A knock sounded at the door, and I got to my feet, leaning in to kiss her forehead before I left her.

"Follow my lead, Rae. Answer the questions." I turned to face her and pointed a warning finger in her direction, fixing her with a serious look. "And for God's sake, remember what I said about honesty. Nothing but the truth, woman."

She squirmed but nodded, and I opened the door, blinking in surprise when I saw not just Seth, but Francesca standing next to him, with tear-stained cheeks. "I'm sorry, Ryder. I'm so sorry."

Fuck.

RAE

When I heard sniffling at the door, and Ryder swearing under his breath, I sat up straighter on the couch and craned my neck, trying to see who it was. I was prepared to deal with whatever happened. I'd experienced a life of misery. I'd learned how to deal with bad situations. And what was the worst my father could do?

I looked at Ryder's honest, handsome face, and I knew exactly what the worst was that he could do. I steeled myself for whatever was going to happen.

"Get in here," Ryder growled, pulling Francesca by the hand and gesturing for his friend to follow suit. "Anne," he said, running a hand through his hair and scowling. "You remember Seth from yesterday?"

Yes, of course, the tall, dark badass who'd helped rescue me.

"Hey," I said with a little wave. He smiled briefly, then resumed his somber expression as Ryder slammed and locked the door, sliding the deadbolt in place. He gave Francesca a pointed look. "Tell me now, what's going on."

She sat gingerly on the couch next to me. "Right after I saw you, I went to donate—Anne's hair."

"You did *what?*" he said. He looked over at me and fixed me with a pointed glare. "You know anything about this?"

Uh oh. I shrank back on the chair and swallowed hard, suddenly remembering just how hard that palm of steel of his was. "Well... I didn't know *much* about it, except that she said my hair could be used for people who had cancer and lost their hair, and I thought it would be a noble cause."

"Oh, great," he bit out. "So we're here pulling out all the fucking stops to save your life, and *you two* think it's the time to start getting all altruistic? Doesn't matter that donating hair that long would draw suspicion from just about *anyone?*"

Francesca's face flushed pink and she wiped tears away, but I didn't want to hear his anger now.

"For God's sake, Ryder, you're overreacting. No one's going to trace me because of my *hair* donation, and anyway, there's no way she's donated it yet. Right, Francesca?" I swung my gaze to hers. "And would you please get a grip? No one's going to accomplish anything blubbering like a fool."

Francesca's jaw dropped and Seth started coughing, but Ryder's tone got my attention.

"I'm overreacting?" he asked, his voice dangerously low. "*I'm* overreacting."

"Ryder, listen," Seth interrupted. "She's out of line and I'm sure you'll show her that, but for now we have to focus on some very important facts. Just listen, okay?"

Ryder's jaw clenched, and he nodded. "Go on."

"It's Dean," Francesca said. The room grew still. I vaguely remembered Dean as the man that had come to my rescue the night before. I'd assumed—perhaps wrongly so—that anyone who'd actually come to the house to drive me home had been someone in Ryder's most trusted inner circle.

"Dean?" Ryder asked, his head tipped curiously to the side.

"Yeah," she said with another sniff. "He saw me in the mailing room downstairs. He saw the bag that I carried and asked me what was in it, and I told him." Her voice dropped. "I know you told me not to say anything to anyone, but I thought that Dean was in the know, so I didn't consider him someone to avoid. But his reaction… it was so strange, sir. As soon as he saw it and I told him what happened, his eyes got all angry, and he took off. I tried to stop him, but he left. And I'm afraid he knows something he isn't sharing with us. Both Seth and I have tried to call him, but he won't answer."

Ryder gave one quick nod, then turned to Seth. "Call the mail room *now*. I'm calling Dean."

Seth slid a sleek phone out of his pocket as Ryder did the same. Ryder dialed, held the phone up to his ear, and pointed a finger first at me, then Francesca. "You two *stay there*," he hissed.

I wasn't going anywhere. Francesca looked like she wanted to die. I wanted to shake her, and tell her to get herself together, but Ryder didn't seem all that enamored by that approach. Instead, I settled on just glaring at her, and she glared right back at me, her arms crossed on her chest.

Ryder hung up his phone after a minute, frowning, and slipped it back in his pocket as he waited for Seth to finish his call. A moment later, we all sat in silence as Seth hung up the phone, shaking his head.

"Sorry, Ryder. Mail pick-up's already come. It's gone into the town delivery system already, which means that it'll be filtered through all of Boston's mail. Can't stop it now. Best we can do is get in touch with the donation center and get someone who works there on our side, looking out for the mail, and covering for us."

Francesca's eyes lit up. "Oh! I know someone. A good

friend of mine works there, and I have no doubt that she'd be able to help."

Ryder nodded, still looking pissed off. "Can you call her?"

Francesca nodded. "Of course."

Ryder turned to Seth. "And you need to track down Dean. Find out what he knows, who his connections are, and if there's been any suspicious behavior the recently."

"Listen, Ryder. I don't believe he knows anything. Swear to God, I'd trust the guy with my life. There's no way he's involved in any way. I mean, he drove the getaway car, man."

"I know he did," Ryder said with a sigh. "That's what concerns me the most. He knows exactly where she came from...." his voice trailed off. "Francesca, make the call and report back here," he ordered. "Anne? You tell us everything you know about the man who kidnapped you."

"He goes by Martel," I said. "He's short, with white hair and is clean-shaven. He's in some kind of monetary business dealings... or something. I was kept in the dark about it all, but I know he loaned people money. That much I could surmise, and I assumed he was a banker or something, before I heard what happens in his office... how he hurts people. He's got scary people who work for him, and they do what he tells them."

Ryder nodded and took a step toward me, his voice lowering. "Has he ever said anything about what he'd do if you left?"

A prickle of fear clawed at my chest. "Yes," I whispered. "He said I would die. And that he'd kill anyone who got in the way of my safety. He's a little... dramatic." My voice dropped off, remembering how he'd shattered the glasses when he caught me in a lie.

"Define *dramatic*," Ryder said, his gaze fixed on me. "You said he never hurt you." His eyes sobered. "Is that the truth? Remember what I said about the truth."

I nodded. "He never raised a hand to me. I mean, he never even touched me. At all. No hugs or anything. But he would have other means of making sure I did what he said."

"Is that right?" Ryder asked. "Like what?"

"Do I have to talk about this right now?" I felt sick to my stomach, and I didn't want to discuss this in front of anyone but Ryder, especially as Francesca's eyes were fixed on me in a way that made me squirm.

"I need details later," Ryder said. "For now, you two have your jobs to do. Seth, make sure the security team is on high alert and don't stop trying to reach Dean. Francesca, you let me know as soon as you hear from your friend at the donation center. Understood?"

They nodded. He got up and opened the door, thereby dismissing them. He shut the door behind them, then turned and faced me.

"You and I are going downstairs," he said. "The more secretive we are about your presence, the more suspicions will arise. But before we do that, we need to talk."

As he prowled closer to me, my heart tapped a crazy beat. At first, I wondered if I was in trouble for something, but he didn't look angry anymore. Just tired.

He sat beside me and took my hand. "Tell me what he did, Rae. I need to know." His voice gentled. "It's just us now. You need to talk about this, babygirl." I liked that.

Babygirl.

I didn't say anything at first, trying to frame how I would tell him, but something about his soothing touch encouraged me.

I took a deep breath. "He wanted me to do what he said, but it was always controlling. Manipulative. No contact with anyone except for the people he employed to come in and teach me, to clean our house, and to cook for us. He wanted

DUNGEON DADDY

me kept pure, he said. And if I did anything he deemed unsafe or disobedient, he punished me."

Ryder continued to trace circles on my hand. I took a deep breath and continued. "He'd... take things away. My favorite toys when I was younger. Privileges, like the TV I was allowed to watch once a week. Desserts. Things like that. But it wasn't like... normal discipline, you know? It was always punitive, but he lectured me, too. He would tell me things about the world outside that would scare me, even give me nightmares. He'd tell me about how poverty-stricken I'd be if it weren't for him. He'd... show me pictures of starving children and drug addicts, and tell me that I'd end up like them if I didn't obey him."

"Jesus."

"Yeah," I whispered. "He's... a scary person."

"Sounds it." He didn't say anything for a time, then when he spoke it was soft. "You know, I'm into this lifestyle so I'm biased, but I can see that this might help heal you."

"I've... read about this as much as I could. I've always been very *attracted* to someone who wasn't controlling me but rather *in* control."

He nodded. "I get that, baby. I do. It's different when it's consensual and with someone you're attracted to. Someone who has *your* best interests at heart."

"That's it," I said. "I know you're right. Ryder, my entire life I've been treated like a child. I don't want that anymore. Please. I want to be treated like a *woman* but free to be who I want to be with you."

He smiled. "Yeah, honey. I'm happy to treat you like a woman." His voice had grown husky.

I scooted over closer to him, needing to feel him, needing for him to touch me again. "Oh yeah? So how exactly might that go?"

His gaze fixed on mine, his eyes heated as he took in

every detail, from the top of my head, down over my breasts, to the fullness of my hips and lower still. He reached a hand out and brushed the hair off my face. "You want someone to take care of you, but you need to know you're in charge the entire time, don't you?"

"Yes," I croaked, as he lowered his hand, brushing the pad of his thumb over my breast, my nipple hardening beneath the fabric. "That's it. Please."

"You want to be able to trust someone who isn't going to hurt you," he whispered. I whimpered a little as he took his hand off me and grasped the edge of my shirt, lifting it. "Arms up, baby," he instructed. I obeyed, needing his healing touch. He divested me of my top and tossed it on the arm of the couch.

"You've got a little birthmark," he said, leaning over and kissing the little mark on my shoulder. "You know, legend has it that birthmarks indicate a past life lived."

I snorted. "I certainly feel as if I've lived several."

He unsnapped my bra, allowing my breasts to swing free. With a sharp intake of breath, his eyes roamed over me. He guided me onto his lap, his erection under my backside as he lowered his head and drew my breast to his mouth, grazing the hardened nipple with his teeth. The quick stab of pain gave way to a sharp wave of arousal at the sensual feel of his warm tongue on my skin. I closed my eyes, my head falling back, and he guided me down to the couch so that I lay flat on my back, a throw pillow under my head. He worked one nipple with his mouth while he flicked the other, then he weighed my breast in his hand, cupping the fullness with his palm as he continued to lick and tease my nipple. He released me briefly, enough to bring his mouth to my ear. "Do you feel like a woman now, Rae?"

I grinned and shrugged. "Not yet."

DUNGEON DADDY

With a chuckle, he tipped me over on my side and whacked my ass.

His voice dropped to a growl. "Lose the pants."

My heartbeat sped up, my palms sweaty, as I tugged my pants off. He gathered up the clothing and tossed it to the floor, eyes on me as he tugged the edge of his t-shirt up. I did what I wanted to do the night before, gently running a finger down the coarse, dark hair thatfeathered down to the edge of his boxers. He let out a sharp hiss, but didn't stop me. After his t-shirt joined my clothes on the floor, he captured my wrists and pinned them by my sides, a spike of fear and arousal followed the loss of control. His mouth came to my ear and he grasped the lobe between his teeth, then ground against me. "How about now? You feel like a woman now?"

"Yesss, Daddy," I whispered, shivering with delight at how good it felt to call him that.

Against my ear, he whispered again. "I know this is new to you."

It was. I was a little embarrassed at how little I knew. For someone who wanted to be treated like a woman, I had a long way to go.

"Doesn't matter," he said. "You'll follow my lead. I'll teach you." He grinned, dropped his mouth to my neck, and kissed me there. A tingle spread along my collarbone and down my body to land between my legs. "What do you say, Rae?"

I didn't say anything, just moaned as he sank his teeth into the tender skin, but a second later he moved his mouth away from me and slapped my thigh. The sharp sting took me by surprise. "What do you say?" he repeated in a husky whisper.

"Yes, Daddy." After the smack, my pussy throbbed and I pushed against him, needing friction.

"Good girl." His mouth came to my neck again, a gentle nip he soothed with a sensual sweep of his tongue, then he moved his mouth past my neck, over my breast, a quick swipe around my nipple causing my pelvis to buck. He kissed the lower swell of my breast, then lower still. He came to the soft skin right above my pussy, and he licked me there. The warmth of his breath tickled me, but also drove me mad, as he left my panties on and kissed my mound. My pelvis rose of its own accord. I needed more. He pressed his tongue onto the fabric of my panties, heat and pressure building. It was unlike anything I'd ever experienced. Alone, in my tower of a room, with nothing but my books and loneliness, I'd explored myself before. But it was nothing like what I felt now. If my self-explorations were a flicker of fire, Ryder's touch was a roaring flame. I would be consumed by the fire and die happy.

"Daddy, please Daddy," I begged as he continued to tease me through the fabric, pressing his tongue on my mound, the heat from his mouth warming me through. He lifted my ass, both hands pushing me upward to his mouth.

"You want Daddy's tongue?"

I could only nod with a whimper. He drew the edge of my panties down only the slightest bit, a centimeter or so, taking the time to worship the small strip of skin he'd bared with kisses and nips. I trembled as he lowered my panties further, an inch at a time, until the tiniest curl showed at the top of my panties.

"This what you want, woman?" he rumbled, his warm breath and deep voice making me tingle. He was so close, and I needed to feel more.

Woman. Yes.

Yes. Hell yes, I was a woman, *his* woman, and he was going to show me what being a woman could be.

"Yes, Daddy. That's it. Please, Daddy. Make me your woman."

He sobered then, lowering my panties until I was bared to

him, lifting first one leg then the other as he divested me of the tiny bit of fabric that kept us apart. Bared like this, I wanted to hide, but my need for him made me feel desperate.

He took my legs and draped them over his shoulders. I knew what he was going to do. I'd read about this, but the sum total of my knowledge of sex having been from the pages of a book, there were gaps. Say, for example, not knowing what this would feel like in real life. How I was to respond. The heroines in my novels seemed to like it. I was game.

I grasped his hair, my fingers weaving through the dark, soft locks as he moved his mouth between my legs and parted my folds.

"Daddy's gonna eat this pussy," he whispered, his breath tickling my sensitive parts. "And you're gonna come on Daddy's tongue, but you're gonna ask for permission before you do. When you're at the cusp, you say *Daddy, please?* Understood?"

I wasn't sure I really knew when I'd be "on the cusp" but I'd give it a shot.

"Let's practice," he growled, his warm breath caressing my skin before he swiped his tongue on my clit. Oh, yes, I wanted this.

"Please, Daddy?"

He grinned, nodded, then lowered his mouth, his hot breath on my folds, but he didn't touch me, not yet. My pelvis rose, as I silently begged for him to touch me. His beautiful blue eyes on mine, his strong, muscled shoulders holding my legs, he drew his tongue through my folds, slowly, like he was lapping the top of an ice cream cone. "Taste so fucking good," he growled, before another long, slow, exquisite swipe of his tongue. He moaned, sucking in my sensitive nub, then releasing me and flicking the tip of his tongue on my pussy once more, each time bringing me closer and closer, a rhythm of soft and sensual and decadent pressure with his tongue, until I didn't think I could take it anymore.

"Please, Daddy?" I whispered. "I'm close." Still meeting my eyes, he pushed his fingers into my core, pumping me while working me up. I lost control.

"That's it," he growled, his voice a deep rumble. "Come for Daddy. Come, baby." My body teemed with pleasure, writhing as his continued to lap at my folds, and when I reached the pinnacle, that sweet moment I'd been chasing, I screamed his name out loud as he held me, drawing every last drop of pleasure from me. I fell back, my legs and back relaxing after the intensity of the orgasm. Slowly, gently, he took my legs off his shoulders and laid them down on the couch. He slid off the couch and came to me.

"Dear God, that was amazing," I said, as he sat on the couch and pulled me into his lap.

"I'm glad. You deserve it. And tonight, I'm gonna make you come again, and again, until you forget everything that troubles you."

I smiled against his chest. "Why? Why me? I don't know much about…things. And I don't know what I have to offer you." My heart still pounded from the climax, but I had questions. "Is this just temporary, me and you?"

A little fear of mine was that he wouldn't find what he was looking for in me. I had no way to reciprocate what he brought into my life.

He was quiet for a moment before he spoke. "See, right there, you're showing me what's special about you. You just tell me how you feel, and don't hold back your fears. I haven't been with anyone in a very long time, Rae. And you're special. There's something about you…"

His erection pressed against his jeans, and I reached a

tentative hand out to stroke him. Would he let me? He groaned as I touched him. I wanted him to feel what I'd felt.

"Tonight," he said. "Tonight when I take you downstairs, I'll make love to you. Tonight, I'll make you mine."

I nodded and grinned at him. I liked the sound of that.

"For now, we get something to eat. I'll see if we have any more developments with Francesca and Seth, and we take it from there. Got it, baby?"

I smiled and nodded, half of me not even caring what happened next. I made my own decisions now. And there would be no going back.

Even if Martel caught me, he could do nothing to me. I was not his child. I couldn't be held a prisoner any longer.

My only real fear now was the retribution he would seek.

Something had to be done.

He was not a man who let anyone take his property without penalty.

RYDER

I HADN'T HELD a woman like this in so long, I almost forgot what it felt like. Having her soft breath on me, her curves pressed up against my body, and her moans still lingering in my ears, I wanted to fuck her senseless, leaving her spent, sated and at my mercy.

But first, I needed to make sure she was fucking safe. In my gut, I felt blowback was coming from having rescued her, and none of the shit that went down with Francesca, Dean, and Seth, made me happy.

"Go get ready to go downstairs, Rae," I said, picking up my phone. "But make it quick. Gonna check to see what's going on, and then we go downstairs. Can't hide you up here any longer. Need to bring you around a bit, have others see you, confirm the rumors that have started. I want them knowing Anne is with me and off limits."

She bent down and gathered up her clothes and smiled. "I'm famished. Sounds good. And I'm happy to parade around with you." When she rose, her chest was still flushed from having climaxed, her eyes still bright. Turning to go, I caught a glimpse of her beautiful, curvy ass. Tonight, I'd paint that ass red, leave my mark, and do it in such a way she fucking loved it. I had a private room that was just mine, fully equipped and immaculately clean. No one, but cleaners had gone there in a year--not even me. It would be perfect.

She spoke over her shoulder as she disappeared around the corner to my room. "I get to walk around with the badass of the club? The one who calls all the shots, and everyone else jumps to listen? *My* boyfriend is the top alpha. Oh, yeah, baby." The door shut with a bang and I sat back, blinking.

Top alpha? Everyone jumps to listen? After I got over her shameless bragging, I couldn't help but chuckle.

I'd show her top alpha.

My phone buzzed, and I glanced at the screen. *Seth.*

"Yeah?"

"Hey. Got ahold of Dean. Not sure what Francesca was talking about. Says when she was talking to him, something clicked and he'll fill you in when he sees you."

"What the hell are you talking about?"

"Gotta ask Dean. I have him here."

"Alright, good. Ra—Anne and I are coming down in a few. Heard anything from Francesca?"

"No, but she felt terrible. She was crying like a baby, and I finally got her to calm down."

For God's sake, I didn't have time for this shit. "Seriously?"

"Listen, boss. I know she annoys you but we have to work with her here."

Like I needed a fucking lecture?

"Tell Dean to meet me in my office in fifteen minutes. Get ahold of Francesca, tell her to be there, too. She's on the floor today and shouldn't be leaving the building until her shift."

"Right. Ok, see you then."

I clicked off the phone, grabbed my t-shirt off the floor, and walked to my room.

She'd left the door to the bathroom open.

Christ.

Steam wafted into the room, but through it I could see her curves, her black hair stark against her creamy white skin. She was soaping herself up. I swallowed hard. I wanted to be the one running my hands all over her body, lathering up her hair, her breasts, her sweet, sweet pussy.

I shook my head.

I had a staff meeting and I needed to dress the part. When I walked the floors of Limits, clients needed to know that I was the man in charge and there would be time for me to indulge in all things Rae later, after I'd made sure she was safe.

I took out a charcoal gray suit and a pressed blue shirt, with a sleek tie that matched, and dressed. I was knotting my tie when she walked in the room wrapped in a fluffy towel.

"Oh. *Oh, God.*" She stood in the doorway to the bathroom, blinking. I turned to face her.

"Yeah?"

"You're... oh wow, you look nice."

I grinned at her. "Thanks, babe. Now get yourself dressed quickly. We have to be downstairs in my office soon."

"I get to go with you to your office? With you dressed to kill, ready to give everyone orders?"

"Yes. But if you don't move, you get to go with me to my office dressed to kill, ready to give everyone's orders, with a suitably sore ass. Got it?"

"Why would you spank me?" she asked, sidling up to me and dropping the towel. Her nipples furled at the cold, her skin still slightly damp. She stepped over the towel and bent in front of me provocatively, wiggling her naked ass up at me as she leaned over and nabbed her clothes. I took the opportunity to give her ass a good, sharp crack.

"I'd spank you for making us late," I said. "Now hurry

it up."

She leaned over and grabbed her panties, making a big show of stepping into them, then grabbed her bra, slowly pulling her arms through the straps and sliding it on. She was cute alright. But enough was enough. When she leaned over to get her jeans, all in super slow motion while I stood there and waited, I'd had enough. I took the flat wooden hairbrush atop my dresser, swung it back, and planted a good hard smack to her ass.

"Ow! Oh, God, that hurts," she said, no longer teasing but glaring at me. I responded with another sharp *crack*.

"Then stop flirting with me and get your damn clothes on."

"I'm not flirting with you! Ow!"

Another hard swat followed the first two. "And that's for lying. Now say, 'Yes, Daddy,' or I'll give you an even dozen right over my knee and this time, you don't climax. You'll sit on a chair in my office on a sore ass." Her eyes flashed at me, but she couldn't fool me. I knew she liked this, and that she needed it from me.

I watched the struggle to obey. She wanted to push me, I could tell, but she hesitated, and I knew she'd felt the sting of the hairbrush. She knew I'd spank her for disobeying me, and she was hedging her bets. I raised a brow at her. What would it be? Obedience, or a spanking?

Finally, her eyes softened, and she stepped into her jeans. "Yes, Daddy."

My cock tightened painfully at her submission, the way her voice softened, her eyes docile. It was beautiful gift she'd given me, and I'd cherish it.

I continued to fix her with a stern look until she'd dressed herself, then gave her a nod of approval. "Good girl. Off we go." I took her by the hand and led her to the door, prepared to show off my new submissive.

JANE HENRY

We took the short trip down in the elevator, and as I walked to my office, I placed her hand on my elbow. "Hold onto me. You don't make eye contact with anyone, not yet, not until I know you're safe. Just stay with me and do what I say."

Limits was only open to exclusive members until five, and then our regular clients would start filtering in. Since we screened all members, we relied solely on fees, and never allowed walk-in clients. In exchange for membership, we provided member with an extravagant, private playground for them to explore their darkest fantasies.

The door to the elevator opened to the main area. A handful of people mingled in the lobby. With Rae holding onto my arm, I nodded to guests as we passed but I did not introduce her. It was better not to, until I came across someone who would want to meet my new girl.

We passed the break room on the way to my office. From the doorway, I could see Caden sitting with a cup of coffee. I waved a hand to him. "Hey," I said. "Caden, this is Anne. She'll be with me, if anyone is looking for her." Caden nodded, his cup to his lips, and gave Rae a salute.

"He's a good guy," I said. "Been on security for Limits since he was out of the Navy six years ago."

Rae nodded but didn't say anything. I cast a quick glance at her. Her face had paled, her eyes bright, but she held her head high. "You're gonna be okay," I whispered. "Just trust me, and stay close. These are good men here to help protect you, too. Caden would never let anyone touch a hair on your head. You're safe, okay?"

She nodded miserably, but didn't respond.

Finally, we took the corner to my office. Dean, Seth, and Francesca all waited in the hallway.

They murmured their greetings, and I pushed the door open to my office, but when I did, I froze. On my desk stood a large arrangement, and as I drew closer I could see it was one of those edible deals, with the melon cut into flower shapes, next to chocolate-dipped strawberries. I turned to the others. "Who put this in here?" I didn't have a secretary, and no one else had the key to my office that I was aware of.

No one responded. Seth's eyes narrowed, and Dean's grew sober, but Francesca just stared in bewilderment, and Rae reached for a chocolate covered berry.

"No. Don't eat that," I ordered. She froze.

Good girl.

"No idea where this came from," I said. "No one put it in here? Well that's strange. Somebody did." The only ones who would know about the surveillance cameras set up in my office area would have been Seth and Dean, and I didn't think it wise to mention anything in front of Francesca.

"There's a card," Seth said, pointing to the arrangement. After a nod from me, he plucked it out. It was attached to a small plastic stick. He handed the card to me.

Owner of Limits. Enjoy your forbidden fruit while it lasts.

Fuck.

"Who was this from?" I asked, looking around. Everyone stared at me blankly. I took the arrangement and put it on the shelf behind my desk, tucking the note in my pocket.

"Call Caden, tell him I want to talk to him," I said. He would be able to run the surveillance cameras, but I didn't want anyone else to know what was going on. Seth nodded, picked up his phone, and placed it up to his ear, walking to the door to make the call.

"Dean. Tell me what's going on. Why did you leave so suddenly this morning?"

Dean sat back in his chair. "Remember I told you the place we went to get her was familiar? I remembered why. When Francesca was talking to me about where she was going, she mentioned Zack, and then I remembered. Few years ago, Zack and I were on our way to Limits. Zack was off duty, but he got a call from a partner. Asked where we were. Turns out they'd gotten a tip from an anonymous caller on a missing person, and witnesses saw him taken by a guy that worked for a man by the name of Martel."

Rae gasped audibly. I swung my gaze to hers, and she'd paled. "That's my father." Her jaw tightened. "Or the man who calls himself that."

I nodded, and we looked back to Dean. "Zack and I ended up driving out to where Rae lives. That's why it looked so familiar. We got nothing, no evidence, and when police went back to investigate they had nothing but the tip. Martel came up crystal clear." He frowned. "I have my suspicions as to why. But the missing person showed up on the news shot dead and buried in the woods not too far from where your car broke down. So I went to Zack."

Seth had come back now, and at Dean's words, Seth froze.

"You went to Zack. Without thinking of talking to me or Ryder first? Are you out of your mind?"

Zack was the head of the local police department, and a former member of Limits. When he'd gotten promoted, he'd left the club but we stayed in touch because he had serious connections.

"What'd Zack say?" I asked.

"Said he'd look into it is all I know. Wish I had more to tell you."

I nodded. It all began to add up in my mind. I had no doubt Martel was a dangerous man. "Francesca? Any luck finding your contact?"

"Yes, Sir," she said with a timid look at me. "I reached my friend at the donation center, and told her not to reveal any information when the package arrived. I also asked that she call me right away if anybody comes asking questions or anything of the sort."

"Good," I nodded, lost in my own thoughts, I stroked my chin when a knock came at the door.

"That'll be Caden," I said, pushing away. I opened the door and stepped out to meet him. "Just a minute, you guys," I said.

Caden stood with his hands in his pockets, waiting for me. I shut the office door, and beckoned for him to come closer. "Hey, man. We've got a situation here. Someone delivered an arrangement to my office, but I have no idea who it was or how it got in there. I have a strong suspicion it's from her father, and I need more info. At this point, I'm not sure who to trust. I need you to reel back the footage from this morning, make note of who got in here, and come and tell me. No one knows you're watching. No one knows what you find, but me."

Caden nodded and gave me a little salute. "Yes, sir."

As he turned to leave both my phone and his buzzed. I glanced at the screen.

Security breach. It was an automated message generated by our security system to alert us that someone other than an outside member had somehow gotten onto our premises.

"Caden, what the fuck is this?"

He shook his head and waved his hand. "Nothing. I was screwing around with the security settings at the back door. I know there's a way to connect to Bluetooth but it's unreliable, so I did another run through and it looks like everyone's getting the error message. I'll clear the history. Just ignore it."

I frowned. It was a hell of a time to be screwing around with security. "You fix that, and no more fucking around with the system." *Jesus.*

He left, and I opened the door to the office, surprised that both Francesca and Rae were on their feet, and Rae was pointing an angry finger at Francesca. Seth was between the two of them, pulling them apart.

"You stay the hell away!" Rae said, when Seth gently pushed her back into her seat.

"What's going on in here?"

Francesca glared at Rae, who returned the same glaring look. "She told me to stop calling you *Sir*," Francesca said. "Said she was the only one that could and since I wasn't your submissive I had to stop acting like it."

I blinked in surprise, and turned to Rae. "Is that true?" I asked.

She frowned. "Yes. And I'm not taking it back."

Seth's brows shot up. I couldn't believe she was behaving this way when so much was at stake. Fuck it.

"Rae, enough. Francesca is well aware of the fact that she's not my sub. And I get why you'd get defensive, but there's no need for you to pick a fight. We all have to be on the same side here."

"Right," Francesca said, hurt clouding her expression. "I'm only trying to help."

"Help? You call drawing attention to us and disobeying Ryder's strict orders *helping?*" Rae got to her feet again. "I had no idea that would be dangerous!"

"Rae, *sit.*"

She did, glaring.

I'd warm her ass for that.

"For God's sake," I muttered under my breath but before I could say a thing, my phone beeped again, at the same time Dean and Seth's did.

I lifted it, only to read a second security message. Fuck it.

"Caden did something with the security alarm. Ignore it."

They both frowned, but I turned back to Rae. I could see why she was angry, and a part of me felt a stab of pride at her ferocity. But still, she had to keep her shit together.

DUNGEON DADDY

Dean's phone buzzed and he glanced at it. "It's Zack, boss."

"Alright. Take the call. I need to check in with Caden in a few." I pointed my finger at Rae. "You're coming with me."

Her eyes were hesitant now that she knew she was in trouble but there were too many unknowns, too much at risk for her to be pulling this shit now. She was a good girl. She'd learn to behave.

She spoke loud and clear but stared at Francesca as she responded way too loudly, "Yes, *Sir.*"

I'd give her another good ten for that, though I had to stifle a chuckle.

I took her by the hand and tugged her along with me, leaving Seth and Dean to sort out whatever other details they could, as I went to meet up with Caden.

"You don't behave that way, little girl," I chided Rae, as we walked along. "There's too much at stake."

"*You* don't see how she treats you," Rae responded. "With those huge, ridiculous puppy dog eyes of hers, all *yes, Sir* and *no, Sir,* and *whatever you want, Sir.*"

I released her hand, spun her around and gave her a sharp crack to her ass.

"Behave yourself," I said sternly.

"You can't do that!"

"Oh yeah? Just did." I pulled her closer and whispered in her ear. "Listen to me. There's a lot at stake here. Getting your panties in a wad because you're jealous isn't going to help anyone."

"Jealous? You think I'm *jealous?*"

"It's crystal clear, babe."

"The nerve!"

"Watch it."

We walked in silence for a moment, her seething beside me and me contemplating the merits of another good spanking. "Need to look at the footage downstairs," I said, not wanting to alarm her.

He knew she was here. He fucking knew. But so far, it seemed he hadn't made a move.

After another moment of silence she spoke up again. "Did you sleep with her?"

"What?"

"Did you sleep with her? With Francesca."

I blew out a breath. "Christ! No, I didn't. Can we please stop talking about Francesca? It's like you've got an obsession."

"She's the one who's obsessed."

"Rae *enough*. And you have no proof of that."

"You wanna bet? You don't see the way she moons over you with those big eyes of hers. Hell hath no fury like a woman scorned."

"*Moons* over me? Honest to God, Rae, no more of this. I don't want to hear it."

She was quiet for a minute. "If I keep talking about her, will you spank me?"

I paused a beat, my jaw clenched. *"Yes."*

She drew a little closer and leaned in to whisper, but I put a finger up to her lips. "Don't push me, babe. You push me now, and you're not going to like what happens. You'll find yourself bottoms up over my knee, and there's no climaxing for bad girls who get their asses punished."

She opened her mouth, then closed it again, then opened it, then shook her head, but said nothing.

"We're going in to take a look at the footage with Caden, or to see what he's found. You'll do what I say and not ask questions. I don't know who to trust here, and I can't make any decisions until I know more information. Okay?"

She nodded. I leaned in and wrapped my hands around the back of her neck, drawing her close to me. I kissed her forehead. "Good girl. You're a very good girl. And remember, there are rewards for good girls at the end of all this."

She sighed, her eyes closed. I pulled away. I needed more time with her, time to kiss her until she was drunk with the taste of it, tie her up and show her what it meant to give control to someone who would take care of her, to spank her headstrong ass and teach her to mind her Daddy. So much time. I needed to get this shit out of the way so I could get to the good stuff.

I input the numbers to the locked door of the surveillance room, and pushed it open. The room was brightly lit, and Caden sat on a swivel chair, not even turning to acknowledge us when we came in. He didn't need to. A full camera in front of the desk showed him who stood there.

"Found who brought your arrangement, boss," he said. "Zack. He came by about an hour ago and delivered it to your desk. Not sure how he got in. I've looked at the footage repeatedly and the best I can guess is that he used your key code. Not sure how he knows it, but you need to reset it as soon as you can."

"Got it." Fucking *hell*. And Dean had gone to him.

"I told you that he has the police department in his pocket," Rae said, wringing her hands. "Ryder, I *told* you."

"And I heard you, but I've had no contact with the police department at all. The only one who has is Dean. Didn't Francesca date Zack a little while back?"

Caden shrugged.

"I've got some digging to do. Alright. I'll get in touch with Zack, and figure out what the hell's going on here. Right now, I've got to get my girl some lunch."

Caden smirked. "This your girl?"

I nodded, feeling a rush of pride as I introduced her. "This is Rae. She'll go by the name of Anne for now. And yeah." I tugged her close and kissed her temple. "She's my girl."

RAE

My stomach churned with hunger. I hadn't eaten since breakfast, and I didn't handle hunger very well. It was likely part of the reason why I'd flown off the handle at the little bitch who called Ryder *Sir*. I mean, it wasn't really like me to lose my temper that easily. Then again, I'd never really had much interaction with other people.

"Thanks for digging, Caden," Ryder said, getting to his feet and taking my hand. He'd called me *his girl* and I still felt a little flush from the memory. "Going to get something to eat."

Ryder ordered lunch to be delivered to his office, and then pointed for me to sit down at a chair by his desk while he made his phone call. "Zack, it's Ryder over at Limits. Got some questions for you. Give me a call."

He hung up the phone. "So how are you feeling right now?"

"Starving. Out of my mind *famished*," I said. "And also, pretty confused. You think the fruit arrangement thing was sent here by Martel? Like a clue he knows I'm here?"

He shrugged. "No idea. Don't want to risk ignoring it,

though."

I nodded. He didn't break eye contact with me, but his blue eyes focused harder on mine. Thinking. Then he lifted a hand and crooked a finger at me. "Come here."

The low, insistent demand made me shiver. I pushed myself to standing, and walked over to him. He swiveled his chair out, and I once again took in his large, muscled chest, the expanse of his shoulders, the way his muscular thighs stretched against his jeans, the flat of his stomach. He patted his knee. For one brief moment, I fantasized about him patting his knee to signal for me to go over his lap. To be punished.

But when I came within arm's reach of him, he leaned back in his chair, and pulled me straight onto his lap. The strong, masculine smell of him, like whiskey and sunshine, filled my senses.

My heart beat a little faster as his hands encircled my waist and rested on my lower back, the warmth of his touch seeping through my clothes.

His deep rumble of a voice arrested my attention, pulling me out of my fantasy.

"I want to hear what you want to know about BDSM. The lifestyle. Scening. What appeals to you, what doesn't. What have you learned from the books you read?

My stomach twisted, my cheeks flaming even hotter. "I don't know if I want to talk about it," I said, feeling a little nervous and shy.

His grip tightened. "Didn't ask you if you wanted to talk about it. I told you to tell me."

I bit my lip, planning my reply, needing to goad him a little. My voice came out in a husky whisper. "And if I... if I don't tell you?"

A muscle ticked in his jaw. "You need to ask?"

I closed my eyes briefly. I knew what would happen if I

didn't. I didn't want to be punished so much as I needed to hear him say it. He'd threatened. Something told me I was fresh out of threats, and soon he'd be making good on his promise.

I swallowed before I took in a deep breath and spoke. "Well, the whole idea of punishment is sexy," I began. "Being punished by someone I'm attracted to like I am to you... the loss of control... the pain that turns to pleasure. There are lots of ways I haven't been spanked, and lots of ways I want to try."

His cock twitched beneath my ass and his eyes sobered. When he spoke, his voice was lower, husky. "You like when I spank you." It wasn't a question because he knew the answer.

At the words, I felt my panties grow damp between my legs, licks of fire stoking the embers of my arousal. "Like what you keep threatening," I whispered. Could I say it? I would try. "Like your... your belt."

He huffed out a laugh. "You're way overdue for Daddy's belt."

I closed my eyes briefly, overcome with warmth and longing.

"I want to try restraints," I said in a choked whisper before I looked at him again. "Cuffs, or rope, or something like that. I'm curious what it would feel like to have no control, so you could do whatever you want to me. And then I... want you to do anything you want to me."

He nodded. "Excellent. Restraints I can do. Go on."

"I want to be punished in front of a room full of people while they all watch."

"Hell yeah. What else?"

My excitement grew, and I felt braver. I looked into his probing eyes, deep and fathomless like the sky at dawn.

"Wax play."

He blinked, startled, and the corners of his lips quirked

DUNGEON DADDY

up. "You want to try wax play? You just jumped several octaves there, babe. And not everything may be as hot as you think when you experience it. A crowded room might overwhelm you, even."

I nodded and swallowed hard, a nervous giggle bubbling up. "I'm curious. With the wax... yes. Just mild... the heat and a little sting of pain... again, your control over me... it sounds... good."

He gently kneaded my lower back. "You're a very good girl. Anything else?"

I had to think a minute. "Well, I am curious about gags, but I'm not sure they'll be my thing. I like... when you lick and bite me, but I'm not sure that's kinky."

He chuckled. "I can make it kinky."

Ohhh. I shivered again.

"Calling you Daddy. That's a big kink."

"Damn right. You do it perfectly."

A warmth of contentment filled me. "And... what about you? What do you want to try with me?"

"I'm a red-blooded male." He chuckled. "I really just want a blow job."

I laughed out loud. "A blow job? I've read about those. I bet I could...learn." My panties dampened at the mere thought.

He reached for my hair and wove his fingers through it, grasping it before he gave it a little tug. "I look forward to teaching you."

My heart pattered in my chest, and when I spoke, I hardly recognized the sound.

"I'd like that," I said in a husky whisper. "When's my first lesson?"

He held onto me and glanced at the clock on the wall behind him. "We have fifteen minutes before our food arrives. Now's a good time."

A spike of fear and exhilaration coursed through me.

Gently, he guided me off his lap. I stood in front of him and his eyes met mine.

His low command made me shiver. "On your knees."

I sank to the floor in front of him, my hands falling to his thighs. I was eager to please him, having climaxed now twice because of him. I wanted to make *him* feel pleasure as keenly as I had. But I was nervous. I felt my eyes grow wide as he nimbly unfastened his belt, the clink of metal giving way to a soft whoosh as he tugged the thick leather belt from its loops. My mouth grew dry as I imagined what he'd do with that belt.

I swallowed hard as I watched him wind the belt around his hand until he'd fashioned a strap. With his empty hand, he freed his cock. I felt both cold and hot as apprehension flooded me.

"Open." I obeyed, shaking a little. He guided his silky, hardened cock into my mouth. He tasted a little salty as my lips wrapped around him and I sucked.

I'd read about this, too. I could at least fake it. I longed to please him.

I gasped as the tail end of his belt snapped on my ass. "Don't stop, Rae. You stop, or disobey me, and I'll whip you with my belt." The sting of pain melted into heat, and as I sucked his cock, I wanted more, needing to please him. His large, muscular thighs fell open, and his eyes met mine. My head bobbed between his legs, my own arousal amping up with every lick and suck.

His nostrils flared, his chest expanding as he barely stifled a groan, reaching for my hair and giving it a sharp tug. He was enjoying this. And *God,* if he was, so was I. Making this strong, stern man groan in pleasure empowered me, my pussy throbbed with arousal.

The belt snapped again on my ass, the sharp crack of

leather making me squirm, my belly dipping. "Good girl," he groaned. He began to tense, his body coiling, and I knew he was getting close. I wasn't sure what I would do at that point. He pulled himself out and I mewled at the loss. He soothed me with the soft stroke of his hand on my cheek.

"That's all for now. You did such a good job, baby. But I need to ease you in. I want to save myself for tonight. I want to be ready for you."

He slipped his hardened cock back in his pants and zipped up.

"Doesn't that hurt you? Don't you need to climax, too?"

He smirked. "I will, babe. You don't worry about me. All you need to worry about is obeying me." He tapped a finger on my chin. "Yes, Daddy?"

I smiled back, flames still licking at my core, my voice husky with want. "Yes, Daddy."

"Good." He pulled me to my feet, laced his fingers around the back of my neck, and drew me closer to him, kissing my forehead before he whispered in my ear. "You're mine, Rae. You came to me because you needed help, and everything you've given me you've given freely. It will take time for us to get to know each other, to know where we go from here. But I take very good care of what belongs to me."

My eyes closed at his words. He was right. We'd only just met, but I'd already given myself to him. I had nowhere else to go and even if I did, I didn't want to. Ours was a special relationship, forged with the bonds of trial and circumstance, but I would do whatever I had to.

I didn't know how to respond, so I didn't even try to censor myself, instead I just spoke what was on my mind. "Thank you, Ryder. For rescuing me. For showing me what my fantasies are like come to life. For giving me a chance." I smiled. "For claiming me as your own."

He pulled me to him in a tight embrace. "When this is all

over? Where you go next or what you do will be up to you. I won't stop you or hold you back. Now it's time for you to find out who you are. But until this is over, and while you're under my protection, I expect you to listen. That way I can protect you and meet your needs."

"Yes." I wouldn't give my submission to a man who hadn't earned it. Ryder made me want to give him everything. "I understand."

A knock sounded at the door as Ryder quickly fixed himself, fastening the belt at his waist.

"Food's here, boss."

Ryder nodded to me. "It's Caden." He opened the door, and Caden came in, carrying a large paper bag, but beside him was someone I didn't recognize, a very tall, burly police officer dressed in a blue uniform with light brown hair, keen brown eyes, and a five o'clock shadow. He looked stern and formidable, and I wondered if he was someone to be trusted. I looked to Ryder to gauge his reaction. He first nodded at Caden to bring the food in, then looked to the officer.

"Zack. Nice to see you."

Zack looked from Ryder to me, then back to Ryder, taking it all in. Though I wore a different outfit, and my hair was cut short, I worried that somehow this man would identify me, like I was on public display. Zack had been the man who put Ryder's arrangement on his desk without permission. If Ryder didn't trust him, neither did I.

"Thank you, Caden. I want you and Seth and Dean to be sure the rooms are set up according to protocol. We have a demonstration in arena one this evening, arena two will be open to the public, and arena three is for a private function, no guests allowed."

Caden nodded. "Got it. Will do, sir."

He shut the door behind him, leaving me and Ryder with a bag of delicious-smelling food, and Zack.

"Zack, have a seat." It wasn't an invitation but a command, as Ryder pulled a chair from his desk and shoved it over to Zack. I hadn't been around people very much, but even I could figure out there was no love lost between these two.

The officer extended his hand. "Officer Zachary Hunter," he said. "And you are?"

I opened my mouth to say "Rowena," when Ryder jumped in.

"This is Anne. She's with me, and I'm training her. She's to listen and not speak. Have a *seat*." Ryder pulled another seat out for me next to his desk and opened the brown paper bag. He removed a clamshell container of salad, opened the salad dressing and poured it on top, gave it all a quick toss with a fork and pushed it over to me. I nodded my thanks, and when he gestured for me to eat, I needed no further encouragement, tucking into the food and listening as the men talked.

"Tell me why you were in my office earlier," Ryder said.

Zack's jaw clenched but his gaze never left Ryder's. "I delivered your arrangement. You're welcome."

"And how did you know the code to get in?" Ryder asked.

Zack rolled his eyes. "The door was already unlocked."

"That's bullshit."

Zack cocked his head to the side. "Is it? So you tell me. How did you know I was here to begin with?"

"Surveillance cameras."

"Naturally. So reel them back further. You're missing something here. I'm not your suspect."

"That's what they all say," I muttered.

Zack's formidable gaze swung to me. "Excuse me?"

Ryder growled, but I continued. "Read a lot of mystery novels," I said with a shrug. "No one ever says, 'Oh! Right! I'm your number one suspect. Thanks for the opportunity!'" I shook my head, ignoring Ryder, who was silently shaking his head at me. "They all deny involvement," I continued. "Sometimes they're telling the truth and sometimes they're not. Gotta keep digging to find out."

Zack's lips pursed then looked back to Ryder. "You let your subs talk out of turn like this, Master Ryder?" He cocked an eyebrow and crossed an ankle over his knee. I wanted to take the rest of my food and toss it into his beautiful, smug face.

Ryder looked at me, his features darkening as he spoke to Zack. "What I allow and do not allow is between me and my submissive, *officer*."

Zack stared at Ryder, but Ryder had eyes only for me, and those eyes were not pleased.

Alrighty then. "Can I have my sandwich, now, please?"

Frowning, he took half a sandwich and handed it to me. I shoved it in my mouth to prevent myself from saying anything else out loud.

"Dean came to me this morning," Zack said. "Wanted to get details on a kidnapping that happened twenty years ago. This have anything to do with you?"

Ryder took a bite of food and shrugged a shoulder. He chewed, and swallowed, taking his time before answering. "I'm not sure if it does or not yet. Go on."

"I looked into it and there was a child reported abducted from a homeless couple twenty years ago. I'm not sure why that information was something Dean picked up on, as we've had countless abductions since then, sadly. But I did want to give him the information I found. We know that it was a newborn baby, and the parents say she had a birthmark on her right shoulder. That's all we've got, though."

The food in my stomach felt heavy.

I turned my face away from him, my heart pattering in my chest, as he continued. "Records show that the parents were poor, and their baby was taken by an infamous loan shark by the name of Frederick Martel, but when detectives went to investigate, they found Martel had legally adopted the child, and there was no verifiable proof that she was kidnapped. He was released, and no one ever saw the birth parents after that."

I'd lost my appetite. I knew that I didn't belong in the home I'd been raised, but the idea of me being someone else's daughter was a difficult concept to grasp.

"Thanks, Zack," Ryder said. He pushed his unfinished food away from the table and looked my way, his blue eyes intense and probing. He wanted to see how I'd react to this news.

I focused on wrapping up the remains of my food, and let Zack and Ryder hash things out. "You have any missing person reports come in recently?" Ryder asked, his eyes on the officer.

Zack shook his head. "I'm not at liberty to discuss those if they *do* get filed, but I can say we haven't gotten any." Zack got to his feet and gave me a long, probing look.

"Gotta get back to the station. Let me know if there are any further developments." He took a slip of paper out of his pocket, scrawled something on it and handed it to me. "My number, if you need it." He nodded to Ryder, and left.

"What the fuck. He gave you his number?" Ryder asked, shaking his head. "Give me that." I felt a stab of pleasure. *He was jealous.*

I unfolded the paper and looked at the number, a series of ones and twos that were easy to remember. "Could come in handy," I said.

Ryder just huffed. He stared, his jaw clenched, his index finger on his lips, contemplative, then he pushed himself to his feet.

"You okay?" He leaned against his desk and loosened his tie, fixing me with the look that made me squirm, and I knew why. I was at the entire center of his attention. His dedicated focus.

"I'm good, Ryder," I said, getting to my feet. Now that I had a fully belly, I had a clearer head, and I knew what I wanted. I walked over to him, taking in his large, powerful form pushed up against his desk with his legs spread, his arms welcomed me. I'd only known him for such a short time, and I already craved him.

When I reached him, he grasped my waist and drew me to him, my front pressed against his torso, hand nestled on my waist. His blue eyes pierced mine and his brows raised as he spoke with conviction. "I'll get to the bottom of what's going on, Rae. He's not going to hurt you. You're safe with me."

"Thank you," I whispered, staring right back at him, and I knew just how to show him I trusted him. "Thank you, Daddy."

His lips tipped up and his eyes warmed. His grip on my waist tightened and he pulled me closer, nestling his chin in my hair. The protective embrace warmed my belly, already my body was trained to respond to being close to him like this. My breasts tingled with the memory of his mouth on them, my pussy pulsed with arousal.

"I'm done hiding, Ryder. I told you I've been treated like a child long enough. And now I want to be treated like a woman." I leaned back and met his eyes. "When do you take me to the dungeon?"

He grinned. "Our guests are arriving. Tonight will be a full house. I had planned on taking you to a private room, but after what you said, I think the dungeon would work. Let's go now." He kissed my head. "It's time to introduce them all to my new submissive."

RYDER

"There are a few rules you need to know, babe," I said, grasping her chin between my thumb and index finger to get her attention. Rae's eyes met mine, heated with excitement and arousal. I could *smell* it on her. It amazed me that someone who'd been away from the world for her whole life would know what she wanted with such conviction.

Then again, maybe that was partly *why* she was so decisive. Her vision hadn't been clouded by the ways of the world. She'd crafted her hopes on fantasy, but there was something endearing about that. What were hopes, if not built on dreams?

"Rules?" she asked. "Dungeon rules. Yes, I've heard about these things."

I chuckled. "Yeah? You're an expert on dungeon etiquette?"

Her face lit up with a grin. "I wouldn't say expert."

"There are two rules I want you to focus on for now. You have to understand that when we go to the dungeon, there are many others there. I know you said you're interested in exhibition, but that'll wait. So rule one. You *never* interfere with a scene. Down in the dungeon, every member is carefully vetted, and it's teeming with security. We run a clean, well-established facility that is one of the most respected BDSM clubs on the East Coast, and there are reasons for that."

She nodded, eager to show me that she was ready to see what she'd been fantasizing about for so long.

"No interfering in scenes. Got it."

I stifled a groan. I doubted she got it.

"People will be down there naked, Rae. Some will be tied to benches, or St. Andrew's crosses. They could be whipped or flogged, and some will be saying *no.* But in the dungeon, no doesn't mean *no.* To many submissives, and even to Dominants and masters, saying "no" is part of the appeal."

She nodded. "And if they want to really stop, they use a safeword."

"Yes. Pick one out for us."

She blinked. "Um. Austen."

"Austen?"

"Yes. When I first saw you, you reminded me of one of Jane Austen's heroes."

Cute. "Okay, then. Austen it is. Now for rule number two." Still holding her chin, I leaned in, my voice deepening. She had to know I meant what I said. "You do *exactly* what I say down there. If you disobey me, I'll *have* to punish you."

"Well I thought that was a given."

I shook my head. "Rae, this is a group of people who are under my authority. Every Dom, Master, slave, and submissive follow a certain etiquette, and I'm owner and head Dungeon Master." I let that sink in. "If you defy me in front of them, you'll leave me no choice. I've given you plenty of leeway. I won't have that liberty in the dungeon."

She shivered a little, and bit her lip, but nodded. "Yes, Daddy."

I nodded. "Good girl. We aren't going to be down there for long, but you'll be submissive to me." I looked down at her clothing. "We need to get you better outfitted for the dungeon, and we will for this evening. For now, you may wear your clothes."

Her mouth dropped open. "For now?" she whispered.

"Yes." I shrugged. "Unless I need to discipline you. But you'll be a good girl, won't you?"

She nodded. "Of course, Daddy."

I called Seth, gave him the code to my place, and asked him to run upstairs grab her a little dress and flats. A few minutes later, he knocked on the door and handed me a bag.

"Thanks, man. Any new developments?"

"Not yet. I'll keep you posted. You on dungeon duty tonight?"

I shook my head. "No, but I'm taking her down to show her around. It's time I introduce my submissive. If we're too walled off, it'll cause suspicion."

"Understood. Let me know if you need anything." Seth left. I knew he'd station himself in the dungeon, just to be on the safe side. The more supervision we had, the better.

I knew I'd be more comfortable when I knew Martel was no longer a threat.

I shut the door after he left, and removed the clothing in the bag. Seth was a smart man. He'd brought a little black dress, sleeveless and short but subtle. She'd fit in without calling attention to herself. She eyed the dress and flats I took out of the bag, her expression a mixture of eager anticipation and trepidation. Good. I didn't want her overly confident going into a place that could take the ground right out from under her.

I loved the dungeon. Part of the reason I'd bought Limits to begin with was because it meant a lot to me to have a safe place where lifestylers could explore their deepest, darkest fantasies and desires. I had a waiting list several hundred people deep, and every single member was rigorously screened. We hadn't had an incident in over four years, and I kept the place under a very closely guarded watch.

She looked about the room, as if looking for a place to dress herself. I tried not to smirk. It was adorable, her thinking she'd have any privacy. She was about to go into the most public place in the entire building, and I'd already seen every inch of her naked body. My cock hardened as I watched her tremble, preparing to be undressed. I would test obedience. I crooked a finger at her.

She eyed me from beneath lowered lashes. "Am I supposed to dress myself, Daddy?"

"You trying to get your ass paddled before we even make it in the dungeon?" She huffed out husky little laugh that made my cock twitch.

"Maybe."

"You know, I think I want a little bit of a strip show. You want some exhibitionism baby? Show me what you got."

Her eyes never left mine as fingered the edge of her top and slowly, with torturously deliberate move moves, lifted the edge of her top, revealing smooth, creamy, lickable skin. I wanted to devour every inch of her. But I'd be patient. It been a long time since I had a submissive. I wasn't going to fuck this up by rushing things.

"That's it, babe. Just like that." I leaned against my desk to watch, my mouth dry as she wriggled out of her clothes. When she'd taken her top off, her hair standing up on end like crazy, I smiled. "Come here."

She walked over me, her expression coy, biting her lip,

and when she reached me, I yanked her closer. She let out a little gasp. I closed the distance between us by wrapping my hand on the nape of her neck and drawing her even closer, capturing her mouth with mine, a clash of lips and tongues that made me crave more of her. I needed to possess this woman who'd come to me for help, who *now* asked me to fulfill her deepest fantasies.

I'd do that, and more.

I halted the kiss with reluctance, wanting to continue but knowing our time was short. I would take her to the dungeon, but we had to go before it grew too crowded. I pulled away, and she fisted my shirt, yanking me closer.

"Whoa, now, Rae," I said, covering my hands with hers. "If we're going downstairs, we need to go. We can't waste any more time up here. There's plenty more time for this."

"I don't want to stop," she said, hitching a knee up on the side of my leg, her front straddling mine. I could smell her arousal in her half-clothed state, sweet and seductive. It took every bit of self-control I had to gently push her away when I wanted so much more. I ran a hand down her shoulder, over the bare skin, my palm scratching over the lacy fabric of her bra. I trailed a thumb over her nipple, just enough to tease her over the fabric. When she whimpered, I pressed a hand to the small of her back, and dipped my hand between her legs, moving my fingers over her jeans, giving her the friction she'd need.

"Ryder," she hissed in my ear. "Touch me."

I smacked her ass. "I am touching you, brat."

"Nooo," she moaned. "Not like that. More. Harder." Her voice dropped to a whisper. "On bare skin." Her begging ended on a near-whine.

I nimbly unfastened her jeans while she panted in my ear, then slid them down her hips. I pulled them to her ankles, bending lower to lift first one foot then the other, then I tossed the discarded jeans onto a pile on the floor. Rising, I dragged my hand along her inner thigh, parting her legs as I stood, then flicked my fingers on the little strip of fabric between her legs. "That's it, babe. Open up those legs for Daddy." She obeyed eagerly, holding onto me for support with her arms wrapped around my neck as I rubbed firmly, drinking in her moans and whimpers.

"You want more?" I asked, working her over good, briskly stroking the fabric.

"Yes. Please," she whispered.

"Good girl. Beg."

I slowed down the strokes and her head dropped to her chest, shaking from side to side. "Nooo. Don't stop!"

I made a low *tsk* sound. If she was going to come with me to the dungeon, she'd fucking remember her place. I pinched her thigh, not hard enough to leave a mark, but sharp enough to get her attention.

"Hey!"

"Enough, Rae. I want you begging me, not ordering me. You'll learn your place."

She closed her eyes briefly, as if willing herself not to snap. The struggle both amused and pleased me. Though she craved what the lifestyle would offer, Rae was not a naturally submissive person. I'd need to train her to listen and obey, but I'd enjoy every *fucking* minute—watching her struggle, then yield to my authority.

I swallowed hard, my cock hardening.

She tossed her head back and inhaled a deep, cleansing breath, her grip around my neck tightening.

"Please, Daddy."

She'd be rewarded for that.

I flicked aside the bit of fabric covering her clit, and slid

DUNGEON DADDY

my finger through her slit. Soaking. "Fuck yeah, baby. So wet for Daddy. So fucking ready."

I stroked upward, just once, then halted, my finger suspended over her most sensitive spot.

"Beg."

"Please Daddy," she panted, her whole body up against me. "I need to climax. Please let me, I'll do anything you ask me to, just don't leave me like this. *Please."*

"Good girl," I said, holding her tight against me, her breath hot on my cheek. I pumped two fingers into her core. She bucked, her pelvis jerking, then with a swift upward motion, I stroked her clit. Her whole body clenched as she rode my hand, her sweet moans urging me to go faster, harder. I held her tight until her knees buckled and she clutched onto me, climaxing against me. I cupped my hand on her ass to steady her, stroking until she finally sagged against me. Nuzzling her fragrant, short black hair, I held the back of her neck, holding her as tightly as I could.

"You please me, climaxing like that."

"Do I?" she breathed.

"So much, baby girl. It shows me that you trust me. That you enjoy being with me. Giving me the gift of your pleasure is something I'll treasure."

I held her in the quiet of the room. I froze when her hand gently grazed my hardened cock, a tentative stroke across the tightened fabric.

"Daddy? May I?"

I pulled her close and kissed her forehead. "Soon. Fuck, yes, soon. For now, we need to get you outfitted for the dungeon."

She stroked one more time, and it took every bit of self-control I had to stop her. "What'd I say?"

She sighed. "You're always pleasing me but taking nothing for yourself. It isn't right, Ryder."

"It is what it is for now." I wouldn't push things with her. "Let's get you dressed. It's time to go down."

I loved the way her cheeks flushed, her chest pink-tinged from having climaxed.

I gently stroked my knuckle across the apple of her cheek. "So beautiful," I whispered, pulling her close to me for a brief kiss to her forehead. "I like the black hair look, you know."

"Yeah?" she said with a smile. "I feel edgy. I'll have to get some piercings or something." Her eyes twinkled as I picked up the black dress and unzipped it.

"I don't think so, babe. You belong to me now. And there's no altering what's mine without permission."

Her eyes narrowed, then softened, and her head tipped to the side. "You're serious."

I gestured for her to raise her arms. "Dead serious. You do anything like that without my permission, I'll spank your ass."

She lifted her arms and I slid the dress over her head. "I'm so plain, though."

Jesus. Plain? "That's like saying they have good art in Rome, or Shakespeare wrote nice plays," I said, with a shake of my head.

She was smiling when her head poked through the top of the dress, and I tugged it down. The fabric slipped over her curves beautifully. I stifled a groan. I'd conditioned myself with years of self-discipline and focus, so that I could train my submissives without taking advantage of them, so that I could build the foundational trust needed. I couldn't ask an educated, competent woman to submit herself to my authority, to obey me and accept discipline, if I didn't hold myself to high standards of self-discipline and integrity.

I spun her around, inspecting her. "Gorgeous," I murmured, giving her ass a sharp crack of approval. "Now for the shoes." I took first one silver flat from the bag and

DUNGEON DADDY

knelt at her feet. She held onto my shoulders while I slipped it on.

"This seems so odd."

"What's that?" I asked, taking the second shoe and slipping it on her foot.

"You kneeling when you're the Dominant."

I looked up from where I knelt beside her and took her hand, bringing her fingers to my lips and kissing them. "Just because you obey me, doesn't mean I don't get to serve you." I stood and said nothing else for a moment, drawing her close. I didn't know what would happen in the dungeon, or even after that, and though I hoped we were on the verge of something great... something lasting, I feared that it would end. We'd come so far so fast.

"Why the hesitation, Ryder?" She paused, and nestled her head against my chest, her hands on my shoulders. "Why do your eyes cloud over sometimes, as if you're upset about something? What troubles you?"

I leaned against the desk and held her, inhaling her beautiful scent, drawing strength from her soft body pressed up against mine. "I'm not new to the scene, Rae."

"Yes. Yes, I know."

"It's been a long time since I've been in this position. My last relationship didn't end well. She left me for another man, and her interests were different from mine. And she never wanted an element of real to all this."

"I don't understand. What do you mean?" She lifted her head off my chest and tipped her head to the side.

"She didn't want a full-time relationship like this. Some submissives and Dominants like to play here in a scene, but their roles don't extend beyond a scene. I wanted more. Full-time." I paused. "Permanent."

She nodded her head thoughtfully. "I don't know much more than what I've read, so I'm not exactly an expert. But I do know that the beauty of this is that there's something for everyone. No?"

I nodded. "Yes." I smiled at her intelligence and intuition. "I agree. The trick is finding someone whose dreams dovetail with your own."

She sobered then, her lips drawing down into a frown. "Is it foolish to hope that my dreams align with yours, Ryder? So soon? When I have no real experience, and we have no idea where we go from here?"

"If it's foolish, then count us both fools, Rae."

She leaned in, her hands gently sliding down my face, and kissed me, a soft, tentative kiss at first that I instinctively deepened, pulling her pelvis against me, sliding my legs apart so I could pull her to me. I slid my tongue gently in her mouth, an exploration, and she welcomed me, her sigh mingling with my moan as we kissed like reunited long-lost lovers, a fusion of hope and passion.

Finally, I pulled away. "It's time I take you to the dungeon, babygirl."

Her eyes lit up, her swollen lips parted in excitement. "I'm ready, Daddy."

She wasn't, she had no idea what she was in for, but I'd help her.

"What are the two rules you have to remember when we go down there?"

"Do what you tell me."

"That's one."

"And..." her voice trailed off and she bit her lip. I crossed my arms and waited. "Uh..."

Taking her by the arm, I spun her around and gave her a sharp crack to her backside.

"Ow!"

"Other couples? Remember?"

"Oh. Right. Never interfere with a scene."

I growled, and took her by the hand. "It's a *major* rule here, Rae. And if you break it, I'll have to punish you in front of everyone -- *severely*."

As soon as I spoke the words, I wanted to take them back, remembering that she'd fantasized about public punishment. "And just because you think that sounds hot doesn't mean that you'll really like it if it happens. Got it?"

"Mm. Okay."

I groaned. She didn't sound so sure at all.

I opened the door to the office. She'd been prepared. She knew the rules. If she broke them, she'd know what to expect.

Caden rounded the corner. "Boss?"

Jesus, I'd almost forgotten all about Caden's instructions. "Yeah?"

He paused for a brief second, his eyes halting on Rae next to me, and I looked at her as if for the first time. Her eyes were bright and excited, her lips full and pink from having been kissed. Her stark hair contrasted with her delicate ivory skin, and the sleek black dress accentuated every curve and angle. She was goddamned *stunning*.

For a brief moment I contemplated hauling her ass back up to my place and keeping her away from everyone, but I'd made a promise to her.

Caden cleared his throat and pulled his eyes away from Rae. "Went through what we discussed."

"Do we need to go back to my office?" I jerked a thumb at the door but he shook his head once.

"No. There's nothing to tell you. Footage from earlier has been wiped clean."

I froze, a cold realization dawning on me. "Is that right?" Someone in my club was tampering with evidence. I needed my staff on, observing everything they could, and my hand went to my phone before I realized that I couldn't call Seth or Dean. And could I even trust what Zack had told me?

"Thank you, Caden. Much appreciated."

"Do we need to go upstairs?" Rae asked.

"No. We're going downstairs. What we need now is time. We'll get to the bottom of this." I smiled at her. "If we bring the focus to the dungeon, whoever is up to something might feel it's safe to make a move." I tugged her hand. "Let's go."

RAE

I walked beside Ryder. I knew I was in trouble. I barely knew the guy, and already, I was falling for him. Every time he issued a command—to one of his staff, or a low growl to me—my heart leapt in my chest. My panties were still damp from climaxing in his office, and I knew he wanted me the way I wanted him. *Inside* me. Alone. I wanted to make love.

When his hand slapped my backside, arousal surged through me like molten lava, steaming hot, and uncontrollable. The way his blue eyes turned stormy or cloudy or hot with arousal made the breath whoosh out of me. His strong, powerful body next to mine made me feel soft and feminine, yet overcoming my inclination to push back against his authority empowered me.

I'd walked out of a nightmare existence and straight into a fantasy. And I didn't trust it. I didn't believe it. It was too good to be true.

"I'll need to check on my crew in a short while, but for now, it's time we enter. Guests are arriving. Stay close to me. And for Christ's sake, Rae." His tone sharpened. "Do what I fucking say."

"We've already established that," I said, a twang of irritation at his harping on about obeying him making my tone snappier than I intended.

"Up against the wall. *Now.*"

The sharp, sudden command took me by surprise. I turned to look at him, but he released my hand, raised a brow, and pointed to the vacant wall of the hallway. My eyes on him, I tentatively walked toward the wall, painted a high gloss black with silver black and white prints scattered throughout. My breath caught in my throat, and I trembled a bit.

He bit out a command. "Face the wall."

I obeyed, my eyes ahead of me on the glossy black wall, my hands placed lightly up against the cool surface. I didn't really know what he wanted me to do.

He stood several paces behind me. Though I couldn't see him, I could feel his eyes on me. I shivered as one minute passed, and then two. "I want you to think about obeying me, Rae. Think about why you want to do this, and what it means for us. Take a few moments to do that."

Alone and vulnerable, he could do whatever he wanted to from his position of power behind me, I did think.

He'd said this would be much harder in real life than in the fantasies I'd had.

He wasn't wrong.

However, it was far better than anything I'd ever expected, and I knew that this was what I wanted—me. Him. *Us.* This dance with the power exchange that challenged me, pushed me, and fulfilled what I craved so deeply.

"Do you want this?"

I jumped. So immersed in my thoughts, I hadn't realized he'd come so close. His breath tickled me, but he didn't touch me. He didn't need to. My body responded unconsciously to his voice, the low, seductive purr making my panties dampen and my breath come in ragged gasps.

"Yes. I want this, Ryder."

A brief pause and then I felt the bottom of my dress lifted before pain blossomed across my ass with a sharp *crack.*

"Then you do what you're fucking told in there."

Immediately humbled and turned on, I nodded. "Yes, Daddy."

He spun me around, wrapped his hand around the back of my neck, and pulled my mouth to his in a kiss that was so deep, so immediately sensual, that my knees buckled. He took what was his.

He released me, took me by the hand, and we marched in silence toward the elevator a few paces ahead of us, me breathless, my heart still racing against my rib cage, him with lips thinned with determination. He pressed a glowing silver circle to take us downstairs, and the doors immediately opened, waiting for us.

He waved me in ahead of him. I stepped onto the elevator. He followed, the doors sliding noiselessly shut, then he pressed a large *D* on the column of buttons, and the elevator dropped with a sharp descent. The walls were mirrored, silver lights illuminating the interior.

"We've come a long way, in a short time," I finally said, breaking the silence.

He looked at me, and one corner of his mouth quirked up. "From you smacking me upside the head with an iron?"

I crossed my arms on my chest. "I meant from you breaking and entering, but whatever."

He smiled, revealing white teeth, his beautiful eyes crinkling at the edges. "I still owe you a spanking for that."

Though I feigned outrage, my heart pitter pattered in my chest. "What? No fair. You've spanked me maybe ten times since then."

"I've given you a few swats here and there. Little love pats, and you deserved it each time."

"Well I'm grandfathered in, because I hadn't consented to your authority at that juncture."

"Oh? That's written in the fine print, is it?"

"It should be!"

The elevator came to a halt and he sobered then, taking me by the hand. "No fine print when I make the rules, baby girl." Before the doors to the elevator opened, though, a high-pitched scream ripped through the air. Ryder froze, my hand in his, as the doors slid open.

"Stay by my side and do what you're fucking told," he said.

Seth jogged past us and a crowd of people gathered around an area. It was hard for me to see what was going on from where I stood, but I heard Seth's deep, booming voice across the room. "Everyone freeze! There's no need to panic. Ryder pushed his way forward. In front of us sat a woman, her knees drawn to her chest. She wore a short black skirt, platform heels, and a bright pink tank top. She was shaking her head from side to side, as if terrified.

Seth crouched down to her and whispered, and Ryder released my hand only long enough to join Seth, beckoning for me to come closer.

"He didn't honor my safeword," she whispered, her eyes closed. "He -- he put the hood on me."

"Sensory deprivation hood?" Ryder asked sternly. She jumped, looked up at him and nodded.

"I didn't know you were here, Master Ryder. Yes. But I couldn't breathe. That was a hard limit. And I safeworded and he caned me for resisting. I was cuffed to the table so I couldn't get away." She shuddered.

"Who did this to you?" Seth asked.

"I don't know who he was," she replied. "I've never seen

him before. When I screamed, one of the guards stepped in and the man ran.

Seth sighed and looked to Ryder, who stood. "Contact Caden and have him see what he can find." He stood. "If anyone else here knows anything that can lead us to the perpetrator, have them let us know right away." Ryder reached for the woman's hand and helped her to her feet. "We're going to get you some help. We have a member here who's a licensed therapist." He turned to Seth. "Contact Rochelle?"

Seth nodded, and offered his hand to the woman, who took it with a grateful sigh. I was close enough to Ryder that I could hear what Seth said when he leaned in close to speak to him.

"Best keep things normal here tonight. Carry on as if nothing happened. My money's on someone trying to make us look bad. Girl's okay, we'll go over footage. Chances are the guy's already left. I'll make sure to call in backup security."

Ryder nodded. "Let me know if you hear anything at all. Got it?"

Seth nodded, and he and the girl took their leave. Ryder turned to the crowd.

"Alright, folks. We'll take care of the disturbance here and make sure all safety precautions are in place. Members are reminded that failure to honor safewords will result in immediate removal from our premises as well as potential charges for assault." He turned and faced the bar. "Drinks on the house for all members."

A murmur of approval went up from the crowd, and soon guests were mingling and making their way up to the bar.

"I'm doing everything I can, Rae," Ryder said to me. "Take a good look around here, and try to relax. Focus on *me*. On doing what I say."

JANE HENRY

I didn't really know what to expect from what I'd read. My understanding was that dungeons ranged from high-end and classy to sordid.

At first glance, it didn't look much different from what I assumed a high-end night club looked like. Dance music played loudly, and a crowd of people danced to the music. Excitement grew in my chest as I walked in with Ryder, his hand on mine firm and heartening. I would not lose my nerve. He leaned in and whispered in my ear, "You're the most gorgeous woman in here, and you belong to me. There is nothing to be afraid of. Just follow my lead."

The first indication I got that something was amiss was when I looked to the left of the large bar. The bartender, a large, muscular man with a shaved head and a tight black t-shirt stretched across his chest, wore a heavy silver cuff around his wrist. When we drew closer, I saw why. A woman on all fours, dressed in nothing but a sheer negligee, knelt at his feet.

God! I inhaled deeply, but kept stride with Ryder as he took a seat at the bar. "The usual for me, a ginger ale for my girl."

I loved when he called me that.

"I'd like something a little stronger," I said, and when his eyes shot to mine, so I tacked on, "Please."

He shook his head. "If I ask you what you'd like to drink, you may tell me," he said, taking the two frosted glasses from the bartender. "Speak out of turn again, and I take you across my knee."

He handed me the drink. He'd spank me for speaking?

I reached for the glass but froze at the look he gave me.

"Did I give you permission to sip that?"

I placed it down on the bar, the glass clinking. Though the sounds around us carried on, I felt as if everyone could hear the pounding of my heart. He leaned in, entwined his fingers in my hair and tugged so hard my mouth fell open, a piercing pain radiating from his touch. "You touch nothing without my permission. Do you understand me?"

Desire licked through me at his utter command. "Yes, Daddy," I whispered, my heart in my throat as tears stung my eyes. I wasn't quite sure why I got all choked up. I *loved* this.

Another tug, and his command rocked me.

"On your knees."

I fell to the floor in front of him, and to my surprise it yielded a bit to my weight. I cast my eyes about quickly, not daring to move my head, and noticed I was by no means the only one on her knees. Clearly, they'd prepared for us.

Ryder took my chin in hand and lifted my eyes to his. "Eyes on me, little girl," he said in a soft, sultry drawl. "You don't look to the side, or away from me when I address you."

I nodded. His voice softened then and he lowered his mouth to my ear. "Baby, your eyes are filled with tears. Remember your safeword and repeat it to Daddy."

I blinked and swallowed, trying hard to calm myself. "Austen,"

"Good," he said. "If you need it, you say it. Understood?"

I nodded. "But you're not even doing anything to me," I whispered. "It would be stupid to use a safeword when we're not in a scene."

His mouth came to my ear one more time. "Baby girl, we've been in a scene since you stepped off that elevator. I am going to tell you one more time. If you need your safeword, use it. Otherwise, I will punish you by not allowing you down here for a very long time. Got it?"

I nodded and whispered, "Yes. Thank you, Daddy."

"Good girl," he said, and that was the last gentle word I got from him. "Back on your stool, now." I felt the eyes of so many around us my cheeks flamed. I'd set foot in the dungeon as the new submissive to Master Ryder, and every single person here knew it. I sat back on my stool, satisfied I'd passed my test, content in the knowledge that I was the property of the most powerful, most experienced Dungeon Master in Limits.

"Eyes to me, Anne." I looked to him, surprised at how weird it was to hear him call me something different. I much preferred *baby*. He held my glass in his hand. "Are you thirsty?"

I nodded. "Yes, Daddy."

"Good. Take a sip." He lifted the glass to my lips and I took a tentative sip, surprised at how the cool, sweet liquid energized me. He took it away and slid it on the counter.

"We'll be back," he told the bartender, then got to his feet and took me by the hand. "I should've gotten a collar to bring with us," he muttered to himself.

I opened my mouth to speak, to tell him that interested me, but a sharp look had me holding my tongue.

"Come with me, babe," he said. "There are things I want to show you."

As he walked he held his head high, as if he were proud of me, and eyes followed us. "Permission to speak, Daddy?"

"Yes?"

I leaned in to whisper. "Why are they all staring?"

"They know me, honey. I'm they're leader. And word is spreading that I've taken another submissive. And also? You're stunning."

It was on the tip of my tongue to counter this comment, but I didn't want to push my luck.

To my right were three men and one woman. I stopped breathing once I realized what was going on. She was laid across the lap of one man, who had his hands up her skirt, while another man knelt behind her and a third plied her with a stout riding whip. Oh my *God*. Her moans and gasps could be heard even from where I stood. What would it be like to have two men pleasure me while one brought me pain?

I glanced at Ryder, who only smirked. "I don't share, kitten."

Though I was a bit disappointed to hear this, a part of me felt a rush of pleasure. I was all his, and he wouldn't share me with anyone.

And I liked "kitten." I smiled at him. "When you call me 'kitten' it makes me want to purr."

The familiar grip on the back of my neck made me shiver. "Believe me. I can take care of you without some other man touching you. And I'd kill any man who tried. *Kitten.*"

Yeah, I could live with the over-the-top possessive thing instead.

As we walked, a sharp cry caught my attention. "No, Master! No!" A woman stood, tied to what looked like a whipping post, her hands bound. She wore nothing but a short skirt and tank top, and a huge man with a large leather paddle stood behind her. He reared back and slapped the paddle against the woman's ass with a crack that made me jump.

"No!" she repeated.

I pulled my hand away from Ryder and turned to the woman, ready to knock the paddle out of the guy's hand. Tears stained the cheeks of the woman bound to the post.

I turned to Ryder. "Do something! She said no!" To my surprise, he didn't stop them but immediately grabbed my arm, pulled me to his torso and whacked my ass, hard, three times in rapid succession.

"Ryder!" Another sharp crack.

"Daddy!" He turned me around.

"You remember what I said. You do not speak to me unless I give you permission. And for God's sake, do not—"

"He's hurting her!"

The noise around us dimmed, and I turned to look at the couple again. I hadn't caught the attention of the large man yet, but the woman's eyes met mine, tear-stained.

"Master," she wailed. "Please, stop!"

And yet the beating went on. She closed her eyes, her wails rising, and I'd had enough. I yanked my hand away from Ryder. He reached for me, but I moved too fast. Dimly aware I'd likely get punished, it was a risk I was willing to take to save the poor woman. How could he allow this to happen in a place *he* owned? I wouldn't obey a man who did that.

Desperate, I shoved him off me and ran to the man with the paddle who was easily twice my size, and kicked him in the shin, hard.

The paddle clattered to the floor. "What the fuck is this?" he said, and the room quieted. The woman turned her tear-stained face to look at me, her jaw dropped, as I reached for her restraints.

"Bitch!" she screamed. "You've done enough. If you release me I swear to God I'll tear your hair out!"

I froze, and everyone around us did at the same time, as Ryder's deep, commanding voice carried across the room.

"Enough!"

I turned to face him, not wanting to, knowing I'd crossed a line I never should have.

God, I'd been so *stupid*.

Never interfere in a scene.

I'd broken rule number one and rule number two.

The Dominant who'd been wielding the paddle turned to me, his eyes dark with anger. "You're with Master Ryder, then? Good." He looked to Ryder, with a small nod of deference before he continued. "Then I know he'll follow protocol."

With dread pooling in my stomach, unable to escape the

inevitable, I looked to Ryder. His eyes were furious, his jaw clenched, his nostrils flaring as he looked at me. "Two rules," he said, low, but it was so quiet in here now I knew that everyone heard him. "Two rules and you broke them both." As he stared at me across the room, I shook. His eyes never leaving mine, he slowly removed his suit coat and hung it on the back of a chair, then loosened his tie. He slid the satin off his neck and unfastened the knot, eyes on me the whole time as a nervous, eager hum filled the room. The clinks of glasses had stopped, even the music seemed softer now, as we took center stage.

He slid his tie into his pocket, rolling up first one shirt sleeve, then the next, revealing strong, muscled forearms. I swallowed. He was going to punish me, here in front of every set of eyes that were on us now.

Not everything may be as hot as you think when you experience it.

Would this be?

There was no doubt in my mind I was going to be punished.

When both shirt sleeves were rolled up to his elbow, he unfastened the thick black leather belt that straddled his hips. My stomach plummeted to the floor at the clink of metal, then the soft whir of fabric as he tugged it free. Forming a loop, he pulled the folded end, and *snap!* The crack of leather reverberated in the room. "Come here."

I don't know how I made it to him with the knowledge of what was to come. When I reached him, he took me by the elbow firmly and marched me toward the bar, making me feel like a naughty girl about to be punished. Though fear zinged through me, I felt a pulse of need between my thighs, a wave of arousal rising.

He's going to punish you.

I tried to talk myself into reason, but I couldn't help it.

People cleared as we neared the bar, and at the very same time my cheeks heated with embarrassment, my breath catching in my throat, my belly dipped with excitement.

"Do you have anything to say for yourself?" He spoke loud enough that anyone nearby could hear him.

"I-I'm sorry, Daddy."

"That's a start." We made it to the bar and to my shock, he cleared it with a sweep of his arm, glass clattering to the floor.

God!

Still, silence surrounded us.

"We'll start with my belt. Hold the ledge and spread your legs."

I closed my eyes and obeyed, gripping the edge for support. A sharp smack hit the side of my legs. I yelped and spread my legs further apart.

"You'll hold position." I gasped as he yanked up my dress, his mouth coming to my ear. "You'll lose your panties. You wanted this, kitten? Let's see how it feels in real life."

He grasped the edge of my panties and tugged down. Oh my *God*. I was bared in front of a crowd of strangers, about to be punished. I closed my eyes, cringing, wanting to *die*, but knowing that the only thing worse than this would be if he *didn't* follow through now. I was heady with arousal and excitement, my legs trembling as I waited for the first sting of his lash.

"We do *not* interfere in scenes in my dungeon," he growled, then *whap!* His belt hit my ass. It burned, and I danced on both feet but didn't have a chance to recover before another stinging *whap!* followed the first. Another smack, then another. I could feel welts rising, the skin throbbing with every lick of his belt, and yet I wanted more. Deep down inside I knew I'd broken the rules, I'd disobeyed him, and obedience was the most important gift I gave him, playing my part in our exchange. I wrestled with guilt, knowing I needed to be punished longer, *harder.*

The smack of leather on naked skin filled the quiet room, and I heard murmurs going up around us. My ass throbbed, arousal dampening my thighs. I could hardly take anymore, each lash driving home both pain and pleasure. Then he stopped. I gripped the edge of the bar for dear life, panting, so close to tears I could nearly taste them, when I heard him threading his belt back on his waist.

"Come here, *now.* You took your first spanking. Now I'll finish what I started."

I turned to him, my ass throbbing from the belting, my knees shaking, all eyes on me. He grabbed a chair, swung it around, and sat his large frame down heavily. Knees apart, he clenched his jaw and pointed to his knee. "*Now.*"

He wasn't finished.

I somehow made my way to him. When I reached him, he tilted his head and pointed once more, indicating for me to lay myself down over his lap. "Two infractions. Two spankings." He lowered his voice. "And when I'm done? There will be one well-behaved little kitten who needs her pussy licked."

My jaw fell open and I shut it quickly, my chest rising and falling with the rapid breaths I took.

"Now, young lady, before I fetch a cane." He shook his head, his lips pursed. "And you don't want a caning over what you just got."

No, I didn't want to find out how that would feel. I ignored the stares and whispers around us as I laid myself straight over his lap. My legs flailed out behind me. He captured them in one swift move, tucking them under his arm.

"You'll take your spanking over my knee for being a naughty girl," he lectured. "A naughty little girl who needs to remember who her Daddy is." His mouth came to my ear.

"That girl *likes* to beg her master to stop. The tears are part of her act. No one's *allowed* to use "no" as a safeword here. You ruined their scene. Because of you, I'll have to issue a credit to both of them for their inconvenience, and re-issue protocol reminders that sub scene interference must be met with immediate punishment. Consider yourself lucky. A Dominant who interferes without good cause loses member privileges."

Without warning, his huge hand clapped on my naked, throbbing backside. It hurt like hell, and I bucked on his lap, swearing out loud, and got another hard swat for that, then another. Swats rained down on my ass and I whimpered, remembering my safeword but *no*, I wouldn't use it, I would not bail the first time he fulfilled my fantasies. I had so many others I wanted him to satisfy. I would take my punishment. I deserved it. I *wanted* this.

Six sharp swats landed on my thighs and ass, one after the other. The spanking burned, it hurt so badly, and he did nothing but spank me. Some swats were lighter than others, as if he was priming me, then *bam!* he took my breath away with another harsher one. The burn and sting pushed me into deep submission. My head swam with the pain and loss of control as he held me tightly over his knee.

"Ten more for your defiance. You will count these for me."

His hand rose and fell with a loud *crack*. "One!" My head felt strangely fuzzy, as I were drifting, floating, and not in the room anymore. Had everyone left?

Another sharp *smack*. "Two!"

I closed my eyes, lost in the moment of pain and pleasure, my breasts brushed up against his sturdy thighs. "Three!"

By the fourth, I tried to speak but something strange happened. I mumbled, but didn't know what I said, I couldn't make sense of the words. The room seemed to fade, and the pain began to lessen. I murmured something incoherent, and my head felt as if it were floating away from my body. Something was shifting. I still felt the whacks of his palm on my naked skin, but I welcomed the pain now, needing more, needing harder, needing to fully submerge myself in this. The last swat fell, and though I opened my mouth to speak, nothing came out.

"Ten," Ryder said for me. He pulled down my dress and swiveled me onto his lap, pressing my head against his chest as he spoke over my head.

"I apologize on behalf of my submissive. I assure you, it will not happen again. Please see Master Seth tomorrow for your compensation."

The large man grunted behind me, but I was only dimly aware of anything except Ryder lifting me up into his arms and walking away. I was floating. Soaring. The crowd had faded, and I heard his shoes clicking on the floor but little else. I could smell him, the clean, masculine scent of wood smoke and pine, and without thinking about it, I burrowed into his arms. My backside throbbed but I was floating, drifting away.

"Are you sorry, baby?" he asked. I tried to respond but the words were difficult to speak, slurred and strangely stuck in my throat.

I nodded instead, and buried my head on his chest.

"Can you speak?"

Yes, I said in my mind but my body wouldn't cooperate.

"Y-yes," I whispered, with difficulty.

I didn't know what was happening to me, but thankfully, Ryder did.

"Shh, baby. Don't say anything. This is where I take care of you now. Ride it, kitten."

Ride it.

I closed my eyes and giggled, though I wasn't amused.

Nothing struck me as funny. I just felt *light.* Free. Everything that troubled me seemed inconsequential. Nothing mattered but me and Ryder, and the ache between my legs I needed satisfied.

"Good girl," he whispered against my ear, his head nestled in my hair. We reached the elevator and he hit it with his elbow. I closed my eyes then, drifting, the feeling of floating exhilarating. I didn't know what was happening, but I didn't need to. Ryder did, and that was all that mattered. He would take care of me.

A vague ding sounded over my head but still, I kept my eyes closed, breathing in his scent, enveloped in his strength and protection. I heard a distant whir behind me, and he stepped onto the elevator.

My belly dipped as the elevator soared upward, my heart pounding along with the need that throbbed within me. I whimpered a little, needing him to touch me, to stroke me, to bring me to climax. He kissed my forehead before his mouth came to my ear, and he took the lobe between his teeth.

"Daddy takes care of you now," he whispered. "Such a good girl, taking her spanking. She's learned her lesson. That's my girl, my sweet little kitten, purring on her Daddy's chest. Such a good girl." He spoke in a low, soothing tone. I closed my eyes as the door to the elevator opened. He stepped into the hallway. I hoped we'd made it to his place. I couldn't bear the thought of being near anyone else right now. I needed to be near him, and hated the idea of anyone else seeing me in this state, whatever that state was. I had no idea, but it felt deeply personal. I had somehow lost control of my reactions.

A low beep sounded and a soft click. I opened my eyes, the lights seeming too bright, so I closed them again and nuzzled back against his strong chest as the door shut behind

DUNGEON DADDY

us. He kept walking, and soon he bent down, laying me gently on his bed.

"I'm taking your clothes off now, Rae. You need to be stripped. Skin to skin contact will be best. I know it's hard for you to talk, so just nod your head for Daddy, okay?"

"Yes," I breathed.

I opened my eyes and took him in, the glorious sight of his tousled dark hair and his intensely blue eyes focused on me with the most tender expression I'd seen. He unfastened the buttons at his collar, then swiftly finished unbuttoning his shirt. He slid out of it, tossing it into a basket by the closet. His white t-shirt stretched across the expanse of his muscled chest. He yanked at the bottom of his t-shirt tucked into his slacks and pulled, yanking the shirt off with one tug. With a quick toss, the t-shirt joined his dress shirt in the basket. Next, he unbuckled his belt. I moaned and shifted on the bed, my head still light, my body floating on air as I watched him pull it from his waist, my mouth dry with the memory of the strapping he'd given me.

"Touch yourself," he commanded. "Stroke your pussy for Daddy, kitten." His low purr of a voice made me shiver as I obeyed, yanking up the dress and sliding my hands between my thighs. My fingers moved easily, my folds slick with arousal. I whimpered as I stroked myself, and he doubled up his belt, giving it a sharp snap before he tossed it. Yes. Fuck, *yes*.

He unfastened his pants, pushing them down his hips. They pooled onto the floor and he stepped out of them, standing in front of me now in nothing but a pair of navy boxers. My hand moved faster, stroking harder, my need rising with every stroke of my fingers taking in his near-naked, beautiful form. He looked like a Greek God. The man deserved legions of angels at his feet. My thoughts swirled rapidly. I couldn't hold a thought, couldn't grasp anything but his gorgeous, strong form and my need to be satisfied.

"Stop." His deep voice halted my stroking. After he was satisfied I'd obeyed, he straddled my body, his large form over me, and I sighed. It was delightful having him straddle me like this, a symbol of his authority. I opened my mouth to speak but once more nothing came.

"Don't try," he whispered, lowering his body onto mine, his strong chest pressed up against mine. "I'm going to strip you now, Rae. I want your naked skin against mine."

I nodded, still unable to speak, but I didn't need to. He pulled me against his chest, holding me with one hand while with the other, he undressed me. Then he tugged the dress past my shoulders, and slid it down. He lifted my pelvis up, sliding the dress off. I still wore no panties, so I lay on his bed with nothing but my bra, which he made quick work of removing.

"That's it, kitten. Bare for Daddy. Shift over, baby." He gently pushed me onto my side and tugged down the blanket. "Get under the covers, Rae. You may feel cold soon, and I want to prepare you."

Why would I feel cold soon? It seemed preposterous. My whole body seemed consumed with flames, my need for him growing with every second that passed.

He pushed down his boxers under the covers and came back to me, gently lowering his body on mine. "Yeah, baby, just like that," he said. I moaned out loud when I felt his warm cock between my legs. He ground himself against me while he held me, his cock sliding against my swollen clit. I groaned, needing more pressure, needing harder and faster.

He lowered his mouth to my ear and I started at the warm, sensual swipe of his tongue against the shell of my ear. "I want to fuck you, Rae. I know you want this, too. Do you want this, kitten?"

DUNGEON DADDY

I could only nod my head vigorously, and respond by letting my legs drop open, welcoming him, begging him to take me. "Ah, that's a girl," he said. "We need to be safe though." He pushed himself up to kneeling and reached over me, his scent enveloping me as he yanked open the drawer next to his bed. I heard a crinkling sound, and a moment later watched as he slid a condom over his hardened cock.

"I'll go gentle."

He held me close and brought his mouth to mine. I felt like a drowning woman finding air, gasping into his mouth, but completely consumed by him, his scent, his strength, his power and control. My need to be claimed by him was the only thing that mattered, and as he kissed me, he gently nuzzled his cock between my legs.

He took his mouth off mine just long enough to whisper in my ear, "Relax. Let me do the work. I'm in charge now, and I'll take care of you." He took both my wrists in his hand and pinned them by my head, pushing his cock deeper between my legs. Pain quickly faded to pleasure as he met my resistance, a gentle but firm thrust that marked me as his. His tongue lapped at my collarbone, then he nipped, as he lifted his pelvis and thrust once more. The tug of pain faded to an electric pulse of need, every thrust bringing me closer to oblivion.

I didn't know I was crying until I felt the soft trickle on my cheek. He kissed my tears away, slowly making me as his, holding me against him, filling me with his presence. "Am I hurting you?" he whispered. I shook my head vigorously from side to side. Hurting me? I'd never experienced such exquisite pleasure.

"Come, Rae. Come for Daddy now. Let yourself go."

Another full, beautiful, powerful thrust, and I shattered, my hoarse scream startling my own ears as I came with abandon. He growled in my ear, dots of perspiration along his strong, muscled shoulders as his whole body tensed with a deep growl, then relaxed, and we came down from climax together, panting into the silence of the room.

He dropped his head to my forehead, his sweet breath coming in gasps, and my arms encircled his neck. I'd wanted him to make love to me so why was I crying? I wasn't sad. I felt free, broken from the chains that bound me, freed from the past that haunted me. I belonged to this beautiful, powerful man who cared for me as if I were the most delicate china, as fragile as spun glass, his precious little girl. I sighed, my tears abating, as I rested in the warmth of his presence.

He rolled over onto his side and brought me with him, maintaining contact the entire time. "Baby, I need to get something to clean us up. Then I need to help you come back from where you were. You don't need to talk. Just trust me. Do what Daddy says, now, and trust me to take care of you." He brushed a final tear from my cheek with a swipe of his thumb. "I'm not leaving you. It might feel like that, but you're okay, kitten. Stay right here. I'll be right back."

He stepped out of bed and I keened at the sudden loss, a small, dry sob escaping me. He walked swiftly to the bathroom and I heard a crank and then rushing water filling the whirlpool tub. A moment later, he came to me and lifted the sheets. I shivered now. I didn't feel cold, but I couldn't stop the shivering, my whole body shaking as he lifted me.

"You're safe, kitten. You're safe now," he repeated, over and over, as he took me to the bathroom, stepped into the tub and drew me in with him. Suds floated around us and the water was so warm it almost stung my skin, fragrant steam filling my senses.

"There, Rae. Rest against Daddy." He sat on a little seat deep in the water and drew me onto his lap, my skin against his, the warm water soothing my shivers.

"Can you talk now, Rae? Try to speak now."

"D-Daddy," I stuttered.

"Good girl," he approved. "Do you feel okay?"

I nodded my head, attempting to speak with an effort. Laughter bubbled up. "I—I—am not sad," I whispered. "I don't kn-know why I cried."

"Shhh," he said. "No more talking now. There will be plenty of time to talk after. I'll tell you what happened. You got to sub-space, kitten. It happens sometimes, though I haven't had the honor of bringing anyone there in a very, very long time."

Sub-space... I had a vague recollection from my books but couldn't seem to remember what it was. "Wh-what is it?"

His voice deepened. "No more talking, now. It's time for you to recover. After you're warmed through, I'll make sure you get something good to eat and drink. All you need to know is that sub-space is an altered state of awareness. It's a sort of state of shock, which is why it was hard to talk. The strapping, followed by the hand spanking, brought you there. I didn't intend it, but it happened anyway." He chuckled. "You were ready for that, honey. Being mentally prepared for a session really helps." He tweaked my damp hair. "You're a brat, you know that? The nerve, heading to sub-space with a punishment spanking."

I laughed out loud, but didn't speak. I wouldn't push the obedience, not after all of that. And now, a funny thing had happened. I *wanted* to please him. I wanted to make him smile. I wanted to hear him call me his good girl and even though I liked it when he punished me, I didn't want him to.

"Time for you to get something to eat," he said, getting to his feet. "Let me grab a towel for you." He stood, reaching for a pair of towels, and I stood with him. He stepped out of the tub, wrapping one around his waist, then stepping down the steps so he stood on the floor. I went to follow him, reaching for my towel.

"Rae, wait for me to help you—"

But it was too late. I didn't know my legs would still be wobbly, and it took me by such surprise, I lost my footing, and went sprawling. He caught me just before my head hit the side of the tub but it was too late. My ankle twisted the wrong way, wrenching pain making me scream out loud.

"Damn it," he swore, lifting me up placing my hands on the side of the tub so he could wrap a towel around me. "Did you hurt yourself? I told you to wait."

"I'm sorry. I was already stepping out. God, I'm such a klutz."

"No, you're not," he said firmly. "You're coming out of sub-space, Rae. You're still shaky from the experience. I should've told you that."

"It isn't your fault." It wasn't. He'd taken such good care of me.

He blew out a breath and tucked the towel under my arms. "You okay now?"

"I think so." I tried to take a tentative step, but when my foot hit the ground my ankle throbbed, pain making me freeze mid-step. "No," I moaned. "My ankle."

He sighed and bent down, wrapping his arm around my neck. "Let's get you in the other room. I'll have to call Caden. He's the only one on staff with medical experience, and I also need to see if he's found anything out about the disturbance earlier."

I nodded miserably but didn't dare make another self-deprecating comment.

After he'd situated me on the bed, he turned to look at me and waved a warning finger in my direction. "I'm going to get you some clothes. Do *not* get up. Am I clear?"

"I won't."

A muscle twitched in his jaw and his brows rose expectantly. "Yes, what?"

"Yes, Daddy."

He left the room and came back a moment later with black lounge pants, a long-sleeved red t-shirt, and a pair of panties. "I'll help you dress, then call Caden." With some struggling, he helped me into my clothes, then quickly pulled on a pair of jeans and a t-shirt himself. He picked up his phone and dialed.

"How's everything going down there?" he asked. "Good. Glad to hear things have settled after the incident we had." He filled in Caden, then disconnected the call and slid his phone into his pocket. "Okay, Caden is on his way up. He'll see to your ankle, and we'll take it from there. Stay put, I'm getting you some food."

A moment later he returned with a tray filled with cut fruit, yogurt, and a bottle of chilled water. "Light but nourishing food is best after you come down from a scene." I wouldn't know, but I trusted him.

"Thank you," I said.

He sat next to me on the bed, watching me, a contemplative look on his face. "I'm sorry about your ankle. But God, Rae, that was a beautiful gift that you gave me." He reached for my hand and squeezed gently.

I put down the spoon to my yogurt and smiled at him. "Thank you, Ryder. It was a beautiful gift that *you* gave me."

His eyes warmed at that, and he brought my fingers to his lips, brushing them softly with a tender kiss, when a knock sounded at the door. "That'll be Caden," he said. "Stay here, hon. I'll be right back."

He left the room, and I heard mumbled voices and the sound of the door opening and closing, then Caden stood in the doorway with Ryder behind him.

"What happened here?" he asked.

"I fell coming out of the tub," I said with a sigh.

"Can you bear weight on it?"

I shook my head.

"Okay. I'll take a look at it but need to speak to Ryder privately first. We'll be right back, okay?"

"Any new developments?" Ryder asked.

"Yeah," Caden responded. "But let's talk in the other room, okay?"

I watched them curiously. Why couldn't he talk in front of me?

"I'll be back, honey," Ryder said, leaning in and kissing my forehead. "Finish your food, and I'll check on you in a minute."

If I knew what was going to happen, I would have kissed him longer, held him back, done anything to stop him. But I didn't know, and neither did he.

"Okay, Daddy," I said, not caring that Caden heard at all. He was, after all, a member of Limits and would've been used to hearing terms like that. But as he left the room, something compelled me to speak out. I didn't care it had been such a short time. I didn't care that Caden overheard. "Ryder?"

He turned to look at me, his damp hair falling across his forehead.

"Thank you."

He grinned at me. "You're welcome. Now be a good girl,"

And he left.

RYDER

⚛

RYDER

"What's up, Caden?" I blinked in surprise as he shut the door to the bedroom. What did he have to tell me that Rae couldn't hear? "You find a way to recover the footage? Find out anything from what happened earlier in the dungeon?"

Caden turned to me, his lips turned down in a frown, and he walked to my doorway. I followed curiously. What was he up to?

"No," he said. "And you won't either."

"Excuse me?" It didn't click, hadn't sunk in yet, when he yanked open the door to the hallway and shoved me out. I stumbled, sprawling onto my hands and knees when a flash of red hair flahsed in my peripheral vision.

Something stung my neck, and I lost consciousness.

When I woke, I opened my eyes, only to see darkness around me. Where was I? I sat up, but pain crisscrossed my eyes, my temples throbbing. It fucking *hurt* like hell. A faint musty smell overwhelmed me, and I opened my eyes despite the pain, holding my head with my hands. My neck still pricked with pain. I rubbed it.

Rae!

I got to my feet, reeling with pain, my stomach churning with nausea. Sudden realizations hit me all at once. Caden had intentionally gotten rid of me. He was in league with someone. But who? The flash of red hair came to my memory. Francesca?

What were they doing to Rae? How would I get to her? My hands clenched into fists as I moved my hands around the small, cramped space. I was locked in a closet, but I couldn't see a thing. I felt around, trying to remember where we had closets and what they contained. There were none on the floor where my apartment was, but there were several on each of the other floor of Limits, mostly utility closets. I spread my hands into the blackness in front of me until I felt the hard surface of a wall. I moved my hands along the smooth finish and moved to my left, trying to find a door. When I hit a corner, I knew I had to go in the other direction. Ignoring the searing pain, I moved as quickly as I could. I had to get to Rae. I had to protect her. I'd kill them, fucking kill them if they hurt her. Adrenaline overcame the pain in my head and neck, I surged forward until I felt it—metal of a doorknob. I tried it, and of course found it locked. But then I remembered that our closets had interior lights. I fumbled around until my hands hit a switch, and flicked it on, bright overhead light blinding me and causing the pain in my head to throb.

I blinked, my eyes adjusting to the light, and looked around me. The room was small, only a few feet wide by a few feet long. A mop and bucket stood in one corner, empty, and a variety of spray bottles and rolls of paper towels stood on a shelf, nothing that would help me get out of here. I looked around wildly, my mind hazy with pain, looking for something that would help me get help from someone outside. I needed to get to Seth. But I found nothing.

Then my eyes settled on a small black box in the corner. I got to my hands and knees and reached for it, ignoring the pulsing in my temples. It looked like a sort of toolbox. I flicked open the latch and my heart soared when I saw a row of screwdrivers, hammers, and nails, a full supply of tools at the ready. I grabbed all the screwdrivers, and moved quickly to the doorknob. Would anyone be standing guard outside the door? What would they do if they heard me?

I found a screwdriver that fit the screws around the doorknob, the nausea that rolled through me slowing me down, until one, two, then three screws fell to the floor and finally, after a few minutes of wriggling and fiddling, the doorknob loosened and fell into my hands. My heart soared as the door swung open, and I assumed a stance, prepared to take on whoever attacked. But no one came. It seemed they didn't expect me to get out so soon, or had only meant to keep me delayed for a short time. In front of me lay a trail of dark red blood, and I brought my hand to my head. I reasoned I must have fallen when I was drugged, and hit my head. Clearly, they'd moved quickly.

My stomach still churning, I knew I had to get to a phone. Mine, of course, was upstairs in the apartment, but I had emergency phones situated on every floor, and every single Dungeon Master had access to the line. That would include Caden, so I had to proceed carefully. It took me a moment to get my bearings. I was on the ground floor, near the dungeon, but on the other side of the large building, where we had meetings. I would be much more effective with help, so I needed to get to Seth, knowing going straight for Rae wouldn't help at all. If they were strong enough to drag me to a closet, there was more than one of them, and what good was I, with no weapons, on the verge of vomiting with every move of my body?

I came to the conference room, pushed open the door, and sank into a seat by the phone. I picked it up, thankful to hear a dial tone, and dialed Seth. He answered on the third ring, and my heart soared.

"Hello?"

"Seth," I hissed into the phone, expecting someone to come barging in any minute. "Ryder. Do not speak my name or let anyone hear you. Where are you?"

"Dungeon."

Thank Christ.

"I'm in the conference room adjacent to The Dungeon. Emergency. Meet me here immediately. Go!"

He clicked off the phone and I waited by the doorway, waiting to hear if anyone was coming, but no one did. A minute later, I heard the pounding of feet running in my direction. I stood against the doorway, hidden in the shadows as they approached. I breathed in relief when I saw Seth's tall, powerful form in the doorway.

"Fuck," he said, his eyes dark, furious. "What the hell happened to you?"

I filled him in quickly. "I need to get to Rae. I have no phone and my head is killing me. Need your help."

"Got your back," he said. "Jesus. Caden?" He shook his head. "Let's go."

He helped me get to the elevator which thankfully still worked, and we pushed the button to my floor, unhindered. I waited for something to happen—for the lights to flicker or the elevator shaft to shake with some interference, but we weren't stopped, and I took the time to tell Seth everything I knew.

I had a whole team that worked for me, but I trusted Seth above all.

"Jesus," he said. "Caden's been dating Francesca on the side. You know that?"

I shook my head. "No idea. Would explain why he was so nasty to Zack."

"I have no idea what his affiliation was, but I know Zack found out that the man who held Rae was a loan shark. Could be that somehow Caden was involved. What would they do to her?"

I shook my head. "They could give her back to him, hurt her, kill her."

The door to the elevator swung open, and we both ran into the hallway toward my entryway. It looked peaceful, the same it had looked after I'd taken Rae up earlier.

"You ready?" Seth said. I nodded, adrenaline surging through me as I punched the numbers into my lock and the lock disengaged. I swung it open, ready to beat down anyone who stood in my way, to rescue my girl. But the curtains swung freely in the breeze, broken glass and shattered picture frames evidence of a struggle. They were gone.

RAE

I FOUGHT HARD, but they overtook me easily, as I couldn't bear any weight on my ankle and it was two against one.

"Ryder will have you locked up for this," I hissed at Francesca as the door to the elevator slid shut. "What did you do to him?"

"Shut up," she said, reaching for her phone and walking over to Caden. "Good thing you're a master at tying knots, sir," she said, giving him a wink. Caden grinned, and my stomach churned, He'd tied my hands and ankles expertly in seconds, and I was powerless to stop him.

"Your father misses you, you know," he said conversationally. "Don't you think it's time we bring you home?"

"You bastard," I hissed. "I want nothing to do with going home. It isn't my home anymore. I'm a grown woman and I've been held against my will. I won't go back."

Caden's eyes darkened. "The hell you won't. I bring you back, and my debt's wiped clean. So don't fuck this up, princess. You do, and you'll deal with me."

A spike of fear caused me to close my mouth. I'd have to be very careful with how I proceeded.

"She's a bitch," Francesca said.

Caden scowled at her. "Do not push it. Not now. You do what I say or you'll deal with me, too." She dropped her eyes and nodded.

"Yes, Sir."

So she was his, then, and she was in this to please him.

"What was it, then, Caden? What clued you in that I was the kidnapped girl who escaped?"

"Be quiet." His gaze shot to me, and I didn't want to push it, fearing that he'd hurt me, or worse, hurt Ryder somehow.

I closed my mouth as the door to the elevator opened and Caden picked me up. "Anyone asks, I'm taking her to the clinic for her ankle," he said to Francesca. "In fact, I want you to spread that rumor. Tweet it, Facebook it, text someone for Christ's sake."

We walked quickly through the dark hallway, but no one really looked our way. The downside of being in a BDSM club with rules like Limits had meant that a submissive being tied up and carried by a Dominant wouldn't arouse suspicion. Francesca began talking to those around us as we went. "She hurt her ankle," "Master Caden is going to fix her up," "Not sure where Master Ryder went."

Caden lowered his voice and whispered, "You fight us, you make a sound, we give orders to kill him."

I stayed silent.

No one followed us but my eyes flitted about the room, and I looked for someone familiar. No Seth anywhere, and Dean was nowhere to be found. We made our way to the exit. As we stepped through the door, a sinking feeling hit my stomach. I wouldn't know where to go from here. He was bringing me back. I'd never escape.

Francesca opened the door to an SUV and Caden slid me in, then they both took their seats, shut and locked the door, and we peeled out of the parking lot.

I knew the direction we were going though I'd only driven these roads once. We were heading back to the prison where I'd been captive my entire life.

"It was foolish of you to donate that hair of yours," Caden said. "He had his cronies looking everywhere, you know. He wouldn't have known where you were. You might've even been able to start an anonymous life. But once he got the word that your trademark hair had been donated, he was easily able to trace back the donation."

I shut my eyes, trying to block out his words. There was nothing I could do to stop this. I would have to escape again, but how? Had he already killed Ryder?

Francesca looked approvingly at Caden. "You're so intelligent, Sir," she murmured, and Caden shot her a smile.

"Couldn't have done it without you. You were the one that pulled it all together."

Of course she had. "So you were the ones that wiped the surveillance cameras?"

Caden grinned. "What do you think? Like taking candy from a baby."

Somehow, I had to get in touch with Seth or Zack. How would I get word to Zack without anyone noticing, though?

And then I remembered. He'd given me his phone number. I pictured the slip of paper in my mind, and could see the numbers in my mind's eye. And if I could notify him without anyone realizing…

We pulled up to the familiar estate, and the wrought iron gate swung open to welcome us, closing shut behind us with a finality that made me sick to my stomach. He was waiting for me. what sort of sick punishment would he give me this time? I had betrayed him so I knew it would be unlike anything I'd ever experienced, and the very thought made me nauseous with fear.

Caden spoke into his phone, and I watched what he did with it.

"You two are so cute together, you know that?" I said, trying to distract them.

Francesca shot me a wary look, but Caden just smiled. "Yeah. We know," he said. I stifled a snort, still watching as he placed his phone in his shirt pocket. He opened the door to the car, and helped me out, cutting off the ties at my ankles. I pretended to bear my weight on my injured ankle, and threw my full body weight at him. Cursing, he stumbled and we fell. I watched his cell phone tumble into the crunchy leaves underfoot. I rolled over, careful to shade his vision, snagged the phone and slid it into my bra, as Francesca ran over to see if he was okay.

But at least now I had what I needed.

I pretended to be docile as I leaned on Caden and he brought me to the house, the front door swinging open. My stomach dropped, and my entire body trembled. He stood in the doorway, his jaw clenched in anger, his eyes like red coals of fury. Behind him, I saw the shadow of his revolver on his desk.

"Welcome home, Rowena." He tipped his head to the side. "What an interesting stylistic change you've made. You're not quite yourself without your long hair, but you know, I'm grateful you were foolish enough to donate it." He spoke to Caden. "Bring her to my office." Then his eyes went to my ankle. "You hurt her? I told you not to hurt her."

"I didn't, no. She injured herself in Ryder's apartment."

Martel's eyes narrowed.

Francesca followed, and I said nothing. Silence was the better option, as he was ready to blow, the slightest provocation at this juncture would be like a match to tinder.

"Is he following? Has he caught the trail yet?" Martel asked Caden.

"Pretty sure he did, yeah. He'll likely come here once he gets out, which was our plan anyway. So far he hasn't reached out to anyone else though. Likely doesn't know who to trust." Caden grinned. "You're welcome."

Martel merely nodded his approval, and pointed to where he wanted me sit.

"I need to use the bathroom," I said, trying to sound desperate. "Please. Send *her* with me for all I care." I'd be mortified having Francesca with me, but she could at least stand outside the door and give them the illusion of supervision.

"Fine," Martel spat out. "Go. And then you get back here. We have much to discuss."

I could imagine what that would involve.

Francesca helped me to the small powder room outside his office. "Don't try anything funny," she said. "I am not going in with you. I can't imagine what you could do in there to get me in trouble, but if you do, I'll hurt you." She said it so nonchalantly, it was as if she were talking about ordering me a cup of coffee.

"I just have to use the bathroom. Not going to do anything cruel and stupid, like other people I know."

She narrowed her eyes and unfastened my wrists. I ignored her and hobbled to the bathroom. I locked the door and lifted the seat, making the sounds loud enough so she could be reassured I was not fooling around. I opened Caden's phone, and hit the text option. The screen lit up. My fingers trembling, I typed in the number I'd memorized.

I've been kidnapped. Ryder is in danger. Come to Martel's residence. Dean knows where it is. Please be quick, and be careful.

I hit "send" and waited until the message showed as sent. Then I stood, tossed the phone in the toilet, and flushed it down, turned on the faucet and washed my hands.

"You'd better not be doing anything stupid in there,"

Francesca said through the door. I opened it, pleased to see she was leaning up against it so she stumbled a bit. Good. The bitch.

"Nothing stupid. For God's sake, I had to pee."

"Give me your wrists," she said, and though her tone was harsh, I could hear the fear in her voice. I'd play with that a little. I needed to have her off her game if I were to escape. Ryder was coming. I needed to play my part.

She reached for my wrists, her hands shaking as she did the knot, so I started, a quick jerk of my hands. She jumped and then glared at me.

"What the fuck was that?"

I shrugged, putting my wrists back out to her compliantly. "What?"

She clenched her jaw. "That—jerky little movement you did."

I leaned in and whispered in her ear. "A reminder that this hasn't even begun. That you're not going to win this and I'll see your ass in jail." I pulled back and gave her my sweetest smile.

She yanked the restraints tighter and pulled me with her, but said nothing as Caden's booming voice yelled out, "Francesca! Where the hell are you?"

She pulled me quicker.

When we got to the office, my father had his phone up to his ear and pointed wordlessly for Francesca to sit me down. I sat, giving her the same knowing grin. She shivered and looked away but stayed right next to me.

"I'm clearing the debt you owe me," he said to Caden. "But you have to help me get rid of Ryder, and the evidence."

I saw a flash of white in the hallway. I stared but didn't show a reaction, just quickly glanced around the room for something that would distract them.

At first I saw nothing, but when I saw the flash again, this time I knew it was Ryder. He'd not come the standard way, up the big driveway but the way he'd come the first night we'd met. My heart surged with hope. He'd climb into my room. He knew the way. He'd come to rescue me.

My job was to keep them distracted.

"He'll come for me!" I shouted, so loudly, Francesca jumped.

I grinned at her. "Skittish, aren't you?"

"Don't talk to her," Caden growled at me.

"You don't want me talking to your precious little bitch?" I asked, hoping to anger them enough that their reaction time would be lessened. "You like bitchy submissives, Caden? Give you more of a reason to spank her?"

Caden took a step toward me as if he was going to hit me, when my father's voice arrested him mid-stride.

"Lay a hand on her and I'll kill you." He laid his revolver down with an audible thunk on the desk next to him. He then turned to me. "You've gotten quite a mouth there, in your time away from home, Rowena." His cold, calculating eyes sent shivers down my spine despite my efforts to be brave.

I swallowed hard. "Something about being held against your will and threatened will do that to a person." I looked at him. "You ought to know."

"I've only ever done what I thought was best for you." He shook his head sadly.

"Bullshit," I hissed, still hoping to distract them. "You did what was best for *you*. And I don't know what your lackeys think they're doing here, but I'll see they pay for this." I knew he was coming. I could feel his presence. Ryder was coming for me. I had to keep distracting them. "You're all going to pay. In fact, you're all so stupid you missed his entrance."

Martel started, and Caden's head whipped around to the

window that overlooked the entryway to the estate. "Ryder's driving through the gates now," I said. "He's coming for me."

It worked better than I expected. The second they were distracted, I shot my foot out and kicked the back of Francesca's knee, making her leg buckle. She screamed, Caden lunged at me, my father sprang to his feet. Francesca turned, her hand raised to strike, but I deflected her slap and shoved her away as hard as I could.

"Don't touch her!" Martel shouted, but Caden ignored him, his large hands grabbing me by the arms. Shots rang out. Caden released me, crumpling to the floor as the door to the office burst open. My heart soared with hope. Ryder came in, followed by Zack, Seth, and several armed officers.

"Weapons down!" Zack roared, his weapon pointed at Martel. Martel didn't listen. Unblinking, he turned the gun to his temple and pulled the trigger.

SIX MONTHS LATER
Ryder

I WATCHED her open the door to the conference room with a smile on her face. Her hair had been returned to its natural blonde, and I loved it. She was the Rae who'd knocked me upside the head with an iron. The girl I'd fallen in love with.

"Good session?" I asked, taking her hand and walking along with her to the hallway that brought back so many memories. Rochelle Knowles, a decade-long member of Limits and licensed therapist, had been seeing Rae weekly in the downstairs conference room now for several months. Some sessions I accompanied her, as Rochelle said Rae was most comfortable around me and I could help her process some of her struggles. But now they frequently met alone, and instead of sessions ending with Rae emerging tear-stained and withdrawn, she often came out smiling now.

"A very good session," she said with a smile. "Though nothing like the sessions I have with my Daddy."

Her fingers entwined with mine, and I gave her a sharp but teasing smack to her backside.

Having a therapist that was a member of the club helped Rae process her own interests and desires without judgment. She had a lot that needed healing. I would help her.

"Rochelle says we can go to every two weeks now," Pride swelled in my chest. Her strength inspired me.

"I'm proud of you. You know that?" I wrapped my hand around the back of her neck and drew her to me so I could kiss her forehead, the move that never ceased to keep her smiling.

"Are you, Daddy?"

"You're a very good girl, Rae," I said, pushing the button to the elevator. The lights ticked down as it descended. "And not everyone could suffer what you have, and rise like you, like a phoenix from ashes."

She sobered, her beautiful eyes meeting mine. "It isn't just me. It's... *You*. This. Us." The doors to the elevator swung open, and Seth stood there waiting.

"Oh, sorry guys," he said. "I was just coming down to check on the conference room. We seemed..." his voice trailed off for a moment before he seemed to remember. "Low on coffee creamer." He cleared his throat.

He exited the elevator and headed left. "Seth?"

"Yeah, boss?"

"Coffee creamer's in that direction." I pointed to the stockroom. He gave me a sheepish salute and turned around.

Rae and I stepped onto the elevator and the doors slid shut.

"He's going to see Rochelle, isn't he?" Rae asked. It was no secret. We'd witnessed her strung up on the St. Andrew's Cross just two nights prior, on the blissful receiving end of Seth's riding crop. Rae was still begging me for such a session but after the spanking I'd given her her first night in the dungeon, I was hesitant. I liked keeping her all to myself.

"Uh huh." The elevator began to ascend. "Seems as if love is in the air tonight."

She snorted. "That's the corniest thing you've ever said."

I whacked her ass. "Watch your tone, young lady."

"Oooh, Daddy, you're so sexy-stern."

"I'll give you sexy-stern right over my knee."

"Oh yeah?" Her eyes flamed, expectant and eager, and she gave me a little shove. I stumbled as the doors to the elevator opened to our apartment.

"Jesus!" I caught myself and nabbed her by the wrist. "Looks to me like someone needs a reminder of her place."

She pulled away from me, but I knew she wanted this. I knew she needed this, the release that would help her forget her pain, and the intimacy that would make her feel loved.

"No. I'm good. I was just teasing you."

"Too late, kitten." I punched the numbers to let us into our apartment, leading her in. I wordlessly drew her into the living room, released her hand, and pointed to the bedroom. "Go fetch the black bag." Her eyes widened as she looked at me. I kept her gaze as I loosened my tie and placed it on the back of a chair. She didn't move.

"Rae, do as I said or you'll get a good taste of Daddy's belt before I even begin."

With a sigh and the most adorable little pout, she did what I asked. I barely stifled a grin. She had no idea I was setting her up.

She returned a moment later with the black velvet bag I kept in the drawer next to my bed. I sat on the couch and rolled up my shirt sleeves. "Come here. Time to tame those little claws of yours, kitten."

She looked at me from beneath lowered lashes, holding the bag out to me. I could feel her already, and knew that if I dipped my fingers between her legs she'd be soaked, her nipples peaked beneath her thin top. I took the bag in my left hand and crooked a finger at her. "Come here."

Dragging her feet, she walked to me and stood between my legs. I drew her onto my knee and nestled her up against my chest. "Let's look in the bag and see what I need today." I unfastened the drawstring and she let out a little sigh. She needed this. But she didn't know what I had planned.

I reached my hand in the bag until I felt the small velvet box. Hiding it in my palm, I drew it out. "What do we have here?" I murmured, opening my palm.

Her mouth dropped open. "Ryder," she breathed.

I placed the bag down and opened the box.

I slid her onto the couch and got to one knee. "Pay attention, babe."

She tossed her head back and laughed, her eyes bright with tears. I reached out and tucked a strand of hair behind her ear. "My brave, beautiful girl. I want to spend every day of my life with you. I want more than your submission, more than your friendship. I want your love, Rae. For eternity. I love you more than anyone or anything I've ever known. Will you please marry me?"

She clasped her hands under her chin. "Yes, Ryder. I love you."

I slid the ring on her finger. "Fits perfectly," I murmured, pulling her to me and embracing her. "Just like you fit perfectly right here."

"Thank you, Ryder. I want to be yours forever."

I smiled at her. "Forever."

EPILOGUE

FIVE YEARS LATER

It seemed as if the warm flicker of candles was what warmed my naked skin, but I knew it was more than that. Ryder's body near mine, and eager anticipation that coiled its way in my belly, heated me through, glowing embers of excitement and arousal.

"Close your eyes," he ordered in my ear, the sound of his voice melodic but commanding. Years of training by his side, and I responded instinctively now.

"Yes, Daddy." I stilled, knowing this was the point where he'd take over, my will melded to his, my every movement aligned to obey. He loved me like this, supple and obedient, eager for his touch and command. Under him, I thrived, happier than I ever thought possible.

Satin slid over my eyes. He gently lifted my head, his hands deftly tying my blindfold in place. The familiar warmth and darkness made me sigh with content, before the snap of a match being struck made me shiver.

Bondage and wax play was his specialty. I was in for a treat tonight.

Though I couldn't see him, I knew what he'd be doing now. He'd tip the edge of the candle so that hot wax fell into his palm, the heat regulated by how high he held it above his palm. He tested everything from floggers to hot wax on himself before he'd allow anything to touch me, and though I'd been christened with wax so many times the sessions blurred in my memory, he still tested first each time.

"Gonna paint that beautiful body of yours," he whispered. "Every inch, dotted with my wax and stripes from the flogger."

I lay spread-eagle on his custom bench. There were many benefits of being married to the owner of an exclusive BDSM club, one being that custom-made furniture and accessories were easy to attain, the other being privacy. This was our room now, one never visited by anyone but us and the cleaners who came every Friday, and it was the dungeon of my dreams. If *Home and Garden* featured BDSM rooms? This one would take the freaking centerfold.

Plush leather furniture, a spanking bench and table fitted with padded straps, a glass case along one wall housing his favorite toys, and hooks along another held every implement he could ever use. The lighting could be easily dimmed or brightened, the temperature adjusted with the touch of a button. Unlike the other rooms at Limits, we also had a luxury bathroom with a whirlpool bath. We made good use of everything.

Without another word, the first hot drop of wax fell onto my skin, a sharp sting rapidly fading to a warm sort of glow, my skin puckering under the quickly hardening wax. Another drop followed another, all along the tops of my breasts and lower still to my abdomen.

Ryder was having fun tonight.

The scent of warmed vanilla filled my senses.

"You know vanilla is an aphrodisiac?" he asked. I jolted at the sudden feel of his mouth at my breast.

"Is it? Like I need another aphrodisiac?" I bit my lip as he pulled my nipple into his mouth and suckled. "Just being around you turns me on."

He murmured approvingly but stopped speaking then, and I felt his warm, probing fingers at my pussy.

"Is my girl wet for Daddy?" He slid his fingers in, groaning. "Fuck yeah. Soaked."

And then he was gone. I mewled in protest but would say nothing more. During a session, he expected perfect compliance. He would make me come—repeatedly—when he was good and ready, but not a second before.

"So beautiful, decorated like this, like sprinkles on a cupcake I'm gonna eat up."

I grinned and held my breath, knowing next he'd clean me with the edge of a knife. He'd never cut me, but I'd still feel the scrape along my naked skin for hours. Knowing he could hurt me but wouldn't turned me on, the play with danger an intimate ride both scary and exhilarating. We'd built a foundation of unshakeable trust.

I started at the first scrape along my skin, and I knew the little hardened drops of wax would be dotting the floor now. I lay as still as I could. If I moved, he could cut me.

"Good girl. That's Daddy's good girl." His murmured approval gave me renewed strength. I could take what he gave me. I would be patient.

I jumped at the feel of his mouth on my nipple once more. He stroked between my thighs, firm, possessive touches making my pelvis jerk. I whimpered, wanting to come already.

He pulled his mouth away. "On your knees, baby."

He helped me flip over onto my knees, my wrists still

free. A sharp crack to my ass made the breath hiss out of me, followed by an order. "Arch that back, belly down. You do not leave that position. Been a while since you've had a good spanking, babe. Don't make it hurt worse than it needs to."

I shivered, waiting for a sound that would clue me in to what he'd use on me.

He moved away toward where he kept his tools, and I keened at the loss of his body near mine. I wanted him near me. Even now, I craved his nearness.

The nightmares had waned from weekly to monthly, now only a few times a year. He always woke by my side, and he'd hold me until my heartbeat slowed and my breathing settled. I rarely dreamed of spattered blood, or locked doors and dark closets any more. I only visited my therapist every month or so, sometimes even skipping months. I enjoyed my job as business manager of Limits, freelance writer, and mom of two, shedding the old skin of my youth and welcoming a new chance at something beautiful. But I still needed him. I still wanted him nearby. And he honored that.

"I'm right here, Rae," he said from across the room.

He knew. He knew I wanted him close once more.

The sound of footsteps approaching made my heartbeat slow as he neared. "Relax. Enjoy the darkness," he whispered in my ear. "Trust me. Do you trust me, baby?"

"Yes, Daddy."

He stepped away, his hand still on the small of my back, then I felt him tense, and a split second later a sharp slap on my backside made me start, the sound of flesh on flesh reverberating in my ears. Before I could recover from the sting, another spank followed and another. He was warming me up with his hand.

When every inch of my skin was on fire, pulsing and stinging, I felt him reach for something else. I braced myself, but when the tongues of the flogger licked my skin,

DUNGEON DADDY

I welcomed them. Bites of leather scattered along my body as he flicked the little bunch of lashes over my ass, my thighs, my lower back. My pussy throbbed, ached for him, with every bite of the leather. Unlike firmer implements that didn't yield, the flogger offered little impact, so he could paint my whole body, my skin glowing, tingling, stinging.

By the time he was ready to fuck me, I'd be primed.

When the smack of one particularly awful stroke caught the tender skin of my inner thigh, I nearly bolted upright but caught myself. If I got out of position, he'd punish me. After five years of marriage to Ryder, I knew he could be very creative with discipline.

Focused effort and deep breathing helped me stay where he'd put me, and the intense desire to please gave me the last bit of strength I needed.

"You wanted to move," he said, his lips against the shell of my ear. "But you stayed in position. You're such a good girl. I love that you let your hair down now, like this. You needed to, baby. Needed to learn to let down your hair. Now look at you, so lovely for me, Daddy's sweet girl." A light lash struck me once more, my skin now flushed with heat. He took my lobe between his teeth and bit down. I squirmed and moaned, as he gentled the nip with the swipe of his tongue, the feel of his mouth on me bringing me closer and closer to climax. One touch of his finger or his tongue, and I would shatter.

"Touch yourself," he ordered.

I stifled a whimper. If I touched myself, I would come, but I wasn't allowed to make myself come. I could edge myself to near climax. I could tease myself and he ordered it regularly, loving watching me work myself to a frenzy. But no. Only Daddy brought me over the pinnacle.

Slowly, I reached for my pussy, my hand shaking as I did

so. One gentle swipe of my finger, and my hips trembled. "Daddy," I whispered. "I'm so close. Please."

His voice hardened and a sharp smack of pain, followed by tingles of pleasure, enveloped me. "Don't you dare until I say."

I dry sobbed against the table in desperation.

"Touch yourself until I say stop." My back arched as something cool stroked the damp skin between my thighs, then my channel stretched and a low vibration hummed. Oh, *God*. Holy *Fuck*. The vibrations continued relentlessly and I did as I was told, stroking myself with firm, rapid movements, not breathing, still plunged in darkness. Pain exploded across my ass, a sharp crack of something hard and unyielding. A paddle? A ruler? Whatever it was, it hurt like hell, but the pain only made me want to come harder, faster, the hum of the vibrator making my breasts swell, the flicks of my fingers over my swollen clit bringing me so close, I couldn't hold back anymore. I didn't care if he whipped me, how he punished me, I had to come, and I had to come *now*. I was beyond the point of being able to stop, my world consumed with nothing but pleasure and pain as the vibrator pulsed, his paddle fell in endless smacks of precision, my hands working between my legs with skill.

"Please, Daddy," I begged. "I'm gonna come. I can't hold back. Please!"

The vibrations stopped. The spanking was over. Something clattered to the floor and the sound of a zipper and the whoosh of fabric made me hitch my breath. God, I was gonna die, but it'd be a happy death.

I felt his warm, hard cock at my entrance, as both of his hands anchored onto my sides. "So fucking wet for Daddy," he grunted. "Hottest fucking thing I've ever seen."

One thrust, and I was undone. The merciful, "Come, now, baby," granted me what I'd been waiting for.

I screamed, my head thrown back as he plunged into me, ecstasy ripping through my body like wildfire. I couldn't breathe, I couldn't speak, my breath was choked out of my body with a low-pitched, near fevered moan. I came so hard my back hurt, tensing as he slammed into me, his hands gripping my hips so hard he'd leave marks.

"Fuck yeah," he growled, then he roared his own release, grunting with primal satisfaction.

He slumped against me and smacked my ass.

"Five years, two kids," he said, panting. "Thousands of spankings, fucked you every which way, more orgasms than there are stars in the sky." He chuckled, bent, and kissed my temple. "And you only get sexier with every day that passes. And I love you more today than the day you said, 'I do.'"

Tears pricked my eyes though I smiled.

"I love you, Ryder. You're so good to me. Thank you, Daddy."

"She's asleep now," Rochelle whispered. I stood in the doorway of Rebelle's bedroom, a warm flutter of happiness washing over me, as I watched Ryder bend over the slumbering form of our little girl. The baby was sound asleep and would likely wake to be fed soon, but our rough-and-tumble daughter was a spitfire who lived up to her name, and bedtime didn't come easily. "I don't think she likes the boxes everywhere."

I nodded, and Ryder joined us, softly closing the door shut. We'd relocated to a larger apartment on the top level of Limits, but had already outgrown it. We'd just bought a house a short distance away and the movers were coming in two days.

To my surprise, I'd inherited Martel's estate, but I wanted

nothing to do with it. I'd taken his money, sold his house, and donated every penny.

"She's like her mama," Ryder said, tucking a strand of hair behind my ear. "Likes consistency and structure and predictability." I felt my cheeks flush a little. Rochelle knew what he referred to.

"Most of us do," she said softly. "But once she gets more space, and a yard to play in, she won't want to come back." She grinned. "And anyway, once she hits her teenage years, the fact that she lives above a BDSM Club might have become an issue."

Ryder snorted. "Uh, yeah. You could say that. Thanks, Rochelle."

When a knock sounded on the door, Ryder nodded. "Seth?"

Rochelle nodded, her eyes alight. "Yep."

We bid them both good night, then Ryder shut and locked the door. "Come here, baby," he said, sitting on the couch and beckoning for me to come to him. I walked slowly, wondering what he had up his sleeve.

"Yes, Daddy?"

I sat on his knee and he drew me to his chest, kissing my cheek and settling his arms around me. "How's that ass of yours?"

"Deliciously tender."

"Excellent."

We sat in the silence for a bit, a deep sense of contentment settling over me. My babies were asleep. I adored my husband. I had everything a girl could ask for.

"Are you happy, Rae?" he whispered.

I lifted my head from his chest and looked into his bright blue eyes, so earnest and loving. "Happier than I ever dreamed possible." I whispered back.

He grinned then. "Breaking down that night was the best thing that could've happened to me."

I grinned back. "I'm still sorry about the iron."

He shook his head.

I sobered then. "Thank you, Ryder. For everything, but especially for showing me that dreams do come true."

THE END

BONUS CONTENT

Beauty's Daddy: A Beauty and the Beast Adult Fairy Tale

CHAPTER ONE (BONUS CHAPTER)

Annabelle

Icy rain whipped my face and hands as I bolted down the length of Main Street. My mind a million other places, I turned the corner and crashed straight into the hugest, most arrogant, pissed-off man I'd ever laid eyes on.

"Jesus!" he roared, lifting the cup up to try to avoid spilling even more, but it was useless. "Watch where the hell you're going!" His deep voice startled me as he looked down from a lofty height, easily a foot taller than I was. So ashamed I could barely look at him, I was only vaguely aware that he looked familiar. He grasped his crushed coffee cup in one hand, a huge umbrella in the other, held so high over my head it did little to stop the downpour. Thick but well-kept stubble lined his sharp jaw, and black hair hung in savage, daring shocks across his forehead.

My mouth dropped open in horror. "I am so sorry," I said, looking around frantically but unfortunately there was nothing along the lines of stray rolls of paper towels or time turners that would help me make this predicament any better. There was just me, a sodden, furious monster of a man, and a few bashful onlookers who went on about their business.

They were smart. He looked ready to kill.

I inhaled, prepared to offer my most sincere apology. He towered over me, easily a full head over my slight 5'1" frame. His hands flicked off excess coffee, while he growled, in a deep, husky, pissed-off voice that sounded more like a growl than polite conversation, "You ought to watch where you're going. For crying out loud, you could've burned yourself." He grunted, attempting to smooth out his clothing, but it was no use. He was a sodden mess. "Did you?"

I blinked. Did I what?

His eyes lifted to mine, brows knit with a furious glare, his lips thinned. "Burn yourself," he spat out.

I looked down at myself stupidly before responding. "No…I'm fine."

"Good," he muttered. "But for Christ's sake, watch where you're going." He turned to leave.

"Mister — whoever —" I sputtered. "I am so sorry I bumped into you like that. Please allow me to compensate you in some way, pay for your dry cleaning, or —"

He turned a scornful eye at me, lips turning down at the edges, his eyes raking me over from head to toe before he scoffed. "You couldn't afford it," he said, before he turned on his heel and left.

My stomach dropped, and then I realized that I was now officially late for work.

"Annabelle!" So much for hoping that Linus, the overbearing owner of Diner on Main, wasn't in yet. "You're late?"

I frowned, turning away from him and hoping he'd get too busy to notice me again, when I heard a voice behind me.

"Do you have any idea who you just slammed into?" Lucy, the local librarian, was all about small town gossip, and knew every single person who ever set foot in any place at any time. She was even tinier than I was, with thick blonde hair pulled into a braid, sporting a short denim jumper. Perched upon a stool at the counter, her blue eyes blinked at me.

"No idea, Luce," I said, stepping out of my rain coat and shaking it off in the back room. "And I don't care. He's the biggest jerk I've ever —"

"*Annabelle!*" My stomach clenched and I barely stifled a groan.

"Good morning, Linus," I said as pleasantly as possible, taking my apron off a peg just behind the cash register and slipping it over my head as Linus came around the corner. Linus — a middle-aged dictator with wire-rimmed glasses atop his too-long nose, a thin moustache and a scant scattering of mud-colored hair across his head, frowned at me.

I fumbled to tie the apron in the back, when Lucy came over and did it for me, leaning in to whisper in my ear. "Don't mind him, honey," she said. "He's in a bit of a temper this morning."

When was Linus not in a bit of a temper?

"Do you know what time it is?" he grumbled, pointing up to the clock.

I can tell time, dumbass.

Releasing a shuddering breath, I nodded. "Yes, sir. 7:07. Looks like my lucky day?" But humor was lost on Linus.

"That'll come out of your pay," he grumbled, as he snatched a wad of napkins from the counter. "Go serve the table with the three kids over there."

I inhaled, shot Lucy a forced smile, and stepped over to the table where three moms with toddlers were having morning coffee. I took their orders, catching a small glass of orange juice before it spilled, and doing my best to put on a smile despite the fact that my head pounded from lack of sleep, my stomach growled in hunger, and I felt like bursting into tears.

I turned to go to the kitchen to place the order with Lucy following me.

"I didn't get to tell you who that was," she hissed in my ear. "It was —"

"Annabelle!" boomed a familiar voice.

Oh, for God's sake.

I closed my eyes, stifling another groan, as Lucy grabbed my hand and squeezed.

Her high-pitched voice piped up. "She's working, Gavin. Bug off!"

I bit the side of my cheek to keep from smiling. I adored Lucy.

Gavin, true to form, ignored her as he plunked down on one of the spindly chairs by the bar. "Cup of coffee, baby," he said. "You know how I like my breakfast." Gavin Montgomery, the local news reporter and small town heartbreaker, flicked his fingers across his cell phone, tipping his head to the side with a cocky grin. He tapped the phone, and a flash illuminated his straight white teeth. As always, he was dressed impeccably, in a tailor-made suit, blue button-down shirt and tie, his hair perfectly coiffed. He was like a small-town Superman in designer duds.

"Selfie of the day, Gavin?" I muttered. "And no, I don't know what your usual is."

Sliding his phone in his pocket, he smoothed out the nonexistent wrinkles from his suit. "Egg white omelette, lean ham, and fruit bowl, baby."

"Linus doesn't carry lean ham, Gavin," I said. "You know what he carries. Standard breakfast sausage and bacon. And I'm not your baby."

Gavin frowned. "All those nitrates. Is he at least carrying free-range eggs yet? Or still in the dark ages?"

"Dark ages."

He shook his head and reached for my hand. His fingers were cold, his palm clammy, and I yanked my hand out of his.

"I'm working, Gavin," I chided. "Let me put in your or—"

But he was too fast. His hand snaked to my waist and pulled me to his side. "I know you're working, baby," he drawled. "But why don't you meet me for dinner tonight? I'll take you to a new little sushi restaurant over the bridge in town. We can drown our woes in sake and get to know one another a bit more."

"I don't like fish, and I despise sake," I lied. Though it was true I hated fish, I'd never tried sake in my life.

He frowned, his pretty blue eyes looking hurt. Damn him. "How could you not like fish?" he said, with a shrug. "It'll help you keep your girlish figure even after you bear children, you know."

My jaw dropped open. "Bear children? I'm only twenty years old, Gavin!"

He shrugged a shoulder, scoffing. "That's perfect. The younger you are when you bear them, the quicker you'll snap back into shape. Why not give it a whirl?"

I pulled away from him. "Putting in your order," I said, ignoring him as he continued to extrapolate on the benefits of women of childbearing years eating fish.

Lucy sidled up to me. "Can I spill his coffee on him?" The reminder of my early morning accident had me groaning out loud.

"God, don't remind me," I moaned.

"Remind you of what?" she asked, but just at then two things happened at once. My phone buzzed in my pocket at the very moment I heard a horrible screeching sound outside the diner, followed by shattering glass, wrenching metal, and shouts coming from outside. I pulled my phone out of my pocket. A text from my sister.

Mom is missing.

A feeling of dread pooling in the pit of my stomach, I tossed my notebook in my apron pocket, and ignoring shouts from Linus and pleas from Gavin, I ran outside with Lucy to see what had happened

My heart stuttered in my chest.

Just around the bend where I'd run into the huge jerk this morning were two cars twisted sickeningly, and one of them I knew all too well: my mom's old navy Buick, the one I'd carefully hidden the keys for the night before. The other? The most expensive-looking car I'd ever laid eyes on.

I raced to the scene of the accident as sirens screamed in the background and onlookers crowded around the cars.

"Mom!" Was she okay? God! She wasn't supposed to drive. She couldn't be trusted not to hurt herself, or anyone else. The dash was demolished, and windshield shattered. Oh, God. If she hurt herself...if she hurt anyone else...

"Annabelle!" My mom's wobbly voice came from the left, and when I turned, my eyes widened in disbelief. No way. No how.

God, *NO.*

My mom stood next to the man whose coffee I'd spilled this morning, his white shirt still drenched with the dark brown liquid. My mother rushed toward me, as his eyes narrowed on mine, his enormous arms crossing his chest.

"Mom, are you okay?" I asked, looking over her frail body. She was still wearing her pale blue pajamas, and a pair of slippers, her gray-streaked hair tied back in a messy ponytail, no glasses in sight. *God.* Where was Melody?

"I'm fine," my mom said, with a wave of her hand. "But *this* one over here thinks it's fine to run stop lights. He ought to be put in jail!" She glared at the man, whose eyes narrowed even further. His jaw clenched as he glared right back at her, pulling his phone out of his pocket and putting it up to his ear. He pointed one angry finger at me, commanding me to stay right where I was.

There was no need. I wasn't going anywhere.

As police cars pulled up with flashing blue and red lights, I grimaced, and a stranger stepped up to me, an elderly woman with a raincoat pulled tight about her. "She's at fault, ma'am," she said. "I saw the whole thing."

"You hush your mouth!" my mom began.

I put a placating hand on her arm. In the early stages of dementia, my mom was in no position to be driving, let alone giving an accurate account of what happened, which was why I'd hidden the keys to begin with. My sister was supposed to be on duty.

"Mom, please be quiet," I whispered, trying my best to keep my cool, when the big beast of a man shut off his phone and stalked over to us, joined by two police officers and a paramedic crew.

His deep voice commanded the situation, as all eyes went to him. "The light turned green, and I began to drive," he said, "when this ancient piece of junk slammed right into my passenger side."

"How dare you call me an ancient piece –"

He held up a hand. "I'm talking about your *car,* not you. Please do not interrupt me. Fortunately, I was alone and it appears no one was truly hurt. The cars, on the other hand, are totaled." His eyes narrowed on me. "Am I to presume that you are the one responsible for this woman?" His gaze wandered over her pajamas and slippers.

I swallowed, embarrassed by my mother's display, horrified at the damage she'd caused, but furious at his dismissal of the one person I loved more than anyone in the entire world.

"Yes," I said, through clenched teeth. "This is my *mother.*" I glared back at him, defying him to insult my own flesh and blood. His eyes narrowed on me, but he said nothing.

"Annabelle," Officer Jones said gently. I went to school with this guy, and knew him well. With a sigh, I looked at him and nodded. "We've talked about this before, okay? Allowing your mother to drive like this, without supervision, is very dangerous."

"Matthew," I began. "I—" but it was too late. My mother heard all.

"How dare you talk about me as if I'm a child?" she said, her voice carrying over the crowd as my hand goes to her arm, attempting to calm her.

"Mom—"

"I am no older than your mother, Officer, and I am perfectly capable of driving. If *this* one over here hadn't been driving like such an idiot, we wouldn't have gotten into an accident!"

I sighed with practiced patience. "Mom, calm down. We need to get you examined," I said, hoping to distract her. I looked to Matthew. "Can we give a report at the hospital?" I asked him.

He nodded. "Of course, Annabelle. I think they both should be checked out. Mrs. Symphony, try to relax, and we'll bring you in to make sure you're okay." He turned to the big guy who was still glowering as if he were ready to breathe fire. "And you, let's get you looked over as well."

I turned my back to both of them, closing my eyes as the paramedics looked over Mom.

His car was worth more than my entire house. How would we ever get out of this?

Read Beauty's Daddy here.

A NOTE FROM THE AUTHOR

Thank you for reading *Dungeon Daddy: A Rapunzel Adult Fairy Tale.* I sincerely hope you enjoyed this book!

Interested in a FREE READ? Sign up for my newsletter here!

What to read next? Here are some *other titles you may enjoy*.

Contemporary romance

Billionaire Daddies Fairy Tales
   *all standalone novels
   Beauty's Daddy: A Beauty and the Beast Adult Fairy Tale
   Mafia Daddy: A Cinderella Adult Fairy Tale

The Boston Doms

A NOTE FROM THE AUTHOR

My Dom (Boston Doms Book 1)
His Submissive (Boston Doms Book 2)
Her Protector (Boston Doms Book 3)
His Babygirl (Boston Doms Book 4)
His Lady (Boston Doms Book 5)
Her Hero (Boston Doms Book 6)
My Redemption (Boston Doms Book 7)

Begin Again (Bound to You Book 1)
Come Back to Me (Bound to You Book 2)
Complete Me (Bound To You Book 3)

Bound to You (Boxed Set)

Sunstrokes: Four Hot Tales of Punishment and Pleasure (Anthology)

A Thousand Yesses

Westerns

Her Outlaw Daddy
Claimed on the Frontier
Surrendered on the Frontier
Cowboy Daddies: Two Western Romances

Science Fiction

[Aldric: A Sci-Fi Warrior Romance](#) (Heroes of Avalere Book 1)

[Idan: A Sci-Fi Warrior Romance](#) (Heroes of Avalere Book 2)

ABOUT THE AUTHOR

Jane is a bestselling erotic romance author in multiple genres, including contemporary, historical, sci-fi, and fantasy. She pens stern but loving alpha heroes, feisty heroines, and emotion-driven happily ever afters. Jane is a hopeless romantic who lives on the East Coast with a houseful of children and her very own Prince Charming.

You can stalk Jane here!
The Club (Facebook reader group)
Website
Amazon author page
Goodreads
Author Facebook page
Twitter handle: @janehenryauthor
Instagram

Manufactured by Amazon.ca
Bolton, ON